future
flash

future
flash

Kita Helmetag Murdock

Sky Pony Press
New York

Sky Pony Press books may be purchased in bulk at special discounts for sales promotion, corporate gifts, fund-raising, or educational purposes. Special editions can also be created to specifications. For details, contact the Special Sales Department, Sky Pony Press, 307 West 36th Street, 11th Floor, New York, NY 10018 or info@skyhorsepublishing.com.

Sky Pony® is a registered trademark of Skyhorse Publishing, Inc.®, a Delaware corporation.

Visit our website at www.skyponypress.com.

10 9 8 7 6 5 4 3 2 1

Library of Congress Cataloging-in-Publication Data

Murdock, Kita Helmetag.
Future flash / Kita Helmetag Murdock.
pages cm
Summary: "Laney can see people's futures when she touches them and has vowed to try to save a new classmate from a fire that is sure to claim his life--and hers"--
Provided by publisher.
ISBN 978-1-62873-822-3 (hardback)
[1. Identity--Fiction. 2. Single-parent families--Fiction. 3. Friendship--Fiction. 4. Clairvoyance--Fiction. 5. Bullies--Fiction. 6. Schools--Fiction.] I. Title.
PZ7.H94197Fut 2014
[Fic]--dc23
2013043263

ISBN: 978-1-62873-822-3
Ebook ISBN: 978-1-62873-953-4

Printed in the United States of America
Cover design by Danielle Ceccolini

For Toby

future
flash

Chapter One

———

MY FIRST MEMORY IS OF THE COLD. I WAS strapped into my car seat, but whatever car I'd arrived in had long since taken off. I don't remember the car or who was in it, just the car seat, rocking back and forth on the stoop. The sky was dark, the road empty, and the concrete front stoop was cracked and icy. I was barely a year old and alone in the world.

Walt doesn't know that I can remember that far back. But I do remember. I remember the scratchy pink blanket and how it hadn't kept me warm even before I kicked it off and out of reach. And I remember Walt, only I didn't know his name yet, walking up the sidewalk and standing in front of me, his breath making puffy white clouds in the air.

"What on earth?" he asked. He looked around but saw that same empty road I'd seen. He stared at me for a minute, shaking his head. Then he picked up a yellow envelope from the stoop and tore it open with his thumb. He pulled out a matching yellow sheet of paper and his face crumpled as he read it. He sank down next to me, facing the road. He held his head in his hands, and I could hear him each time he exhaled, blowing out the cold night air with force, as if to rid it from his body.

When he finally stood, his eyes were red, and he stuffed the envelope and paper in the pocket of his navy blue parka with shaky hands. He considered me for a while, adjusting his baseball cap a few times as if maybe that would solve something. Then he took his parka off and placed it over me.

As soon as his warm hand touched my arm, I closed my eyes and saw an image of the future flash before me. It was the first time I can remember that happening, which is probably why I remember the day on the stoop so well. There is a certain clarity to the present on the days when I see the future—the days when I have what I've come to call a *future flash*.

It was a quick image and, though it would happen eleven years in the future, it was as clear as the stars above me. I saw Walt and me, sitting at a kitchen table together, drinking coffee and hot chocolate and eating muffins. I knew right then that I didn't have to worry about being left out in the cold anymore, and I giggled with relief. Walt looked down at me and smiled. When I didn't stop, he started laughing, too. Then he brought me into his green wooden house. The house I now call home. We've never talked about that night or how I know that he found me on a stoop and that he's not really my dad.

I mention this today because this morning Walt and I are eating some of Carmen's blueberry muffins and drinking coffee and hot chocolate at the kitchen table and everything, down to the stain on the left sleeve of my black hoodie to the crumb of muffin on Walt's chin, looks exactly as it had when I saw it all those years ago. That's how I know something important is going to happen. Whenever I experience one of my future flashes, it means I'm going to have an interesting day.

Of course, at the moment Walt is making the

morning as boring as possible by drilling me on fraction problems at breakfast.

"You know this one, Laney," he says, giving me an encouraging smile. But I've been thinking about car seats and cold nights and have no idea what he asked.

"Don't worry, Walt. I studied this time," I reply, gulping down the end of my hot chocolate before slinging my backpack over my shoulder. I lean over to brush the muffin off his chin and kiss his scratchy cheek. "Just wish me luck!"

"You don't need luck, Laney. It's all up here," he replies, tousling my hair.

I tug at a piece of my short ink-black hair. "Really? Math is in here?"

"Ha-ha. Get to school or you'll miss the test."

Chapter Two

———

I F I CUT THROUGH THE FIELDS AND FARMLAND behind our house, the walk to school should take fifteen minutes, but I always end up stopping at Tabitha's along the way. She has dozens of cats, all females, and they lounge on her back porch in the sun like ladies by a pool, only moving to roll over and stretch from time to time. On an early fall day like today, Tabitha's usually out there too, watering some of her plants, with at least one cat twirling around the mismatched socks on her feet.

"Good morning, Laney!" she calls out, her purple glasses flashing in the sun. "Come sit and have some tea with me and the girls!" Tabitha can't remember that I need to go to school, even though I tell her every time I stop by her house. I pause next to her porch to scratch a skinny gray-and-white-striped cat with a crooked tail.

"Is this one new?" I ask her.

"Got her at the shelter yesterday," Tabitha says, brushing back a wisp of her long blue-gray hair. "One of these days they're going to cut me off, but you know I just can't stand to think of them in those cages." The small cat licks the back of my hand and begins to make a rumbly motor sound.

"What's her name?"

"Why don't you name this one?" Tabitha offers, leaning down to water a row of potted herbs.

"Really?" I scoop up the feather-light cat. She climbs up my shirt and onto my right shoulder. A print of my favorite Frida Kahlo painting hangs on the wall of my tree house, the one where she looks stately with two parrots in her arms and two on her shoulders.

"How about Frida?" I suggest.

Tabitha looks up from her watering. "It's different. I like it."

Frida nibbles at a piece of my hair.

"Come sit for a while," Tabitha insists.

"I've gotta get to school." I gently pull Frida off my shoulder and place her on the porch. She protests with a loud meow before joining the other cats. I imagine a different day ahead of me, one where I skip school and sit in the sun with Tabitha and her cats, sketching pictures of the cats in my notebook while Tabitha drinks lavender tea and embroiders on the porch. Instead I wave goodbye and continue on my way through the field to school, the right shoulder of my sweatshirt dusted in gray fur.

It's not until I'm almost there that I remember Mrs. Whipple's announcement yesterday about getting a new kid in our class. This has never happened, as far as I can remember. Thornville is a sleepy town of just over a thousand people and Thornville K–12 is the town's only school. I've been in class with the same seven boys and four girls since Kindergarten. Nearly all of their parents work for the chicken factory and it's the kind of job you take because you grew up in Thornville. No one moves here hoping for a better life.

I drag my feet, even though I'm already at risk of arriving late. When I meet someone for the first time,

I almost always have a future flash. This can be fun or unsettling, depending on what I see. I try to think optimistically. Maybe I'll see a future friend. Against the odds, I hope for a girl, one who loves art and who comes from somewhere exotic and far away from Colorado—somewhere like Los Angeles or New York City. I imagine seeing a future flash of us spending our afternoons together in my tree house, painting and drawing. Of course I'd have to take down all the pictures of my other future flashes. I wouldn't want to explain those to anyone. But I'd take them down for a friend.

When I get to our classroom, the boys are beside themselves with excitement. They're hoping for another boy, of course. They talk even louder than usual and keep eyeing the door. Their dream of having an even number of boys for their football games at recess could finally come true.

When the bell rings, everyone rushes to find a seat. One seat remains empty.

"Where's the new kid?" Axel shouts, and just like that the door opens.

The new boy stands in the doorway with an apologetic smile. He's no football player. His scrawny body would be better suited to stand in for the goal post. He's wearing a gray T-shirt with the periodic table of elements on the front and bright orange hair sticks up all over his head. As if that wasn't enough to place him permanently on Axel's bully list, he's covered in freckles. I mean *covered*, like he was dipped in butter and then rolled in a bowl of freckles. For a moment everyone is so fascinated with his freckles that they don't recognize that this is not what anyone was hoping for. Then he sneezes. Twice. And it's like someone let the air out of a balloon. The whole class deflates.

"Oh, maaan," Axel groans, putting his face down on the desk. Mrs. Whipple shoots him a dirty look. He bangs his head against the desk until she raps on it with her fingers and tells him, "Enough."

"This is Lyle," Mrs. Whipple announces. To her credit, her toothy smile never wavers.

"Hi guys," he greets us with a little wave before walking over and sinking down in his seat. Mrs. Whipple doesn't bother with further introductions. Even she knows it would be painful for everyone involved.

Instead, she says, "Welcome to seventh grade, Lyle!" Then she faces the board and points to our schedule. "I'm sure you're all happy that you have P.E. first period today. So, before you get too settled in, let's line up and head down to the gym!"

I glance at Lyle as I stand up. He's taking his time to push in his chair. I'm pretty sure he's not happy that we have P.E. first period, but he shouldn't worry too much. Once he meets Ms. Fontane, he'll realize that our gym class is not going to test his athleticism.

Lyle catches me looking over at him and I avert my eyes, pretending I meant only to check the clock above him. I feel bad for him, the new boy who knows he's already a disappointment to everyone. I dread seeing an image of his future because it can't be good. Not that I'll be getting near him anytime soon. The last thing I need to do is connect myself to the boy who's bound to be Axel's newest punching bag. Axel has already secured my position at the lowest rung on the social ladder by calling me Insane Elaine and Art Freak since Kindergarten. I've learned to fly under his radar and befriending Lyle would not help.

Ms. Fontane is waiting for us in the gym. Not your

typical gym teacher, she weighs at least three hundred pounds and hates sports. She manages to breathe heavily and sweat profusely even when just watching other people exert themselves, and she usually spends the whole gym class sitting on the side of the gym, fanning herself with her hand. The only exercise she approves of is dance. So while I imagine other kids across the country learning to kick a soccer ball or shoot a basket in their gym classes, we have spent the last few years learning pliés and the box step, while the basketballs gather dust in a bin in the corner.

"Today we will be learning to square dance!" Ms. Fontane announces as we file into the gym. The entire class groans. "Find a partner," she instructs before slumping into her favorite metal chair. The chair creaks under her weight.

There is a quick scramble and of course I am left facing Lyle, whose frown suggests he's as horrified as I am at the prospect of dancing together. I avoid eye contact by taking a sudden interest in what all the other students are doing. Most of them are standing in square dance position, holding their partners' hands, looking bored. Axel slouches against the wall, smirking. I bet he's appreciative of Lyle right now since an uneven number of students means that he gets to sit this one out. Ms. Fontane reaches over and turns on the boom box. While the rest of the world has advanced to iPods and other digital music systems, Ms. Fontane uses the same giant boom box with the same cassette tapes that she's been using for the last twenty-five years.

"Now, we're going to start with swings and then we'll move on to do-se-do! Okay, everyone face your partner and grab hands!" she shouts over the music.

Lyle puts his hand up. I hesitate.

The music stops.

"Elaine! Grab your partner's hand!" Ms. Fontane yells. She reaches back over to the boom box and the music fills the room again.

I reluctantly put my hand back up. Lyle grabs it with his hand, which is surprisingly dry and warm. I close my eyes. What I see is worse than I ever could have imagined.

Chapter Three

———

MAYBE IT'S BECAUSE OF ALL HE'S SEEN AS a volunteer firefighter, but Walt has always been adamant that I stay away from fire.

"Laney, you have to remember that even a controlled fire is a dangerous fire," he used to say when I asked him why the wood-burning stove in our house sat empty all winter or why we dealt with the cold night air on our camping trips by hopping into our sleeping bags early rather than lighting a bonfire. He doesn't need to remind me anymore. After all of his warnings, a mere lighted match can make my stomach clench.

When I touch Lyle's hands, I am engulfed in flames.

I can't breathe. Smoke sears my lungs. I squint, trying to make out my surroundings. Smoke is every-where. *I can't breathe.* My heart pounds with this realization. Bright patches of fire dance on the floor around me. There's something or someone lying in a pool of blood on the floor. I can't see clearly through the smoke.

I cough and cough but can't get the smoke out of my lungs. Frantic for oxygen, stumbling forward, I claw at the air.

Where am I?

Then I see Lyle in the haze ahead of me, his bright hair the color of the fire around him. There's blood all over his gray T-shirt. His nose is swollen to nearly twice its normal size and his eyes are puffy and black. He's trying to tell me something, but I can't hear him over the roar of the fire. The heat presses down on me. I stumble forward, desperate to understand what Lyle's saying, but as I do I trip over something soft on the ground in front of me. My hand reaches out to stop my fall, landing on a patch of fire. The heat scalds the skin on my palm.

I push myself up, screaming.

"Laney!" Lyle cries, his voice finally reaching me above the din of the fire.

I can't take it anymore. I push past him, away from the fire.

Then I remember to open my eyes.

I gasp for breath and find that the air is cool and thick with oxygen. I want to cry with relief because, for now, I am safe. Lyle is safe too, though his skin is fire-truck red under his freckles. He pulls his hands away from mine and claps them behind his back. It takes me a second to understand that I'm still in the gym and am supposed to be learning how to square dance. The entire class is staring at us.

"What's going on?" Ms. Fontane barks, her finger on the pause button.

I'm not sure, so I don't know how to answer. Some of the students begin to snicker. Two girls have their hands over their mouths and their wide eyes stare at me as if a third eyeball has sprouted on my forehead.

Did I scream out loud?

"I don't feel so well," I say, looking down at my Converse sneakers. They are covered in drawings of Tabitha's cats—only on my sneakers the cats are red and blue and yellow. I remember my impulse to stay on her porch this morning and imagine myself drawing in the sun, far away from the gym and the heat of everyone's stares.

"I should guess not after that display," Ms. Fontane sighs. "Honestly, Elaine. You can sit for a moment, and Axel will take your place."

As we've had more boys than girls in our class from the beginning, the boys are used to pairing up for dancing. But even in my shaken state, I feel terrible for exposing Lyle to Axel this way on his first day of school.

"I'm okay," I try to say, but the words come out as a choked whisper. Axel smirks at me.

If you don't know Axel and you take a look at his big blue eyes, white blond hair, and skin as pale and smooth as a baby's butt, you might think he is an angel, the kind of kid who holds the door for old ladies and always remembers to say *please* and *thank you*. You'd be wrong. He's the meanest kid in the whole school.

As if he can read my thoughts, Axel knocks his shoulder against mine when we trade places. *Sorry,*

Lyle, I think, but I'm relieved to lean against the cool concrete wall. My mind feels scrambled and I need to collect my thoughts. I sink down to the floor and pick at a string on my shredded jeans as the music begins.

What *was* that? What did I see? I check my hand for burn marks. It felt so real. My hand looks the same as always, the skin on the back covered in ink doodles, my bitten fingernails coated in chipped black polish. I study my palm. No burns. I shiver and draw my knees closer to my chest, thinking of the flames and the blood.

I hear laughter and look up. Axel has grabbed Lyle's hand and is shaking all over and opening his mouth as if in a scream, though no sound is coming out. Axel's long legs and arms are flying this way and that, out of control, as if he is having some sort of seizure. Is that what I looked like? Poor Lyle steps back, biting his lip. What a first day. I'm sure he wishes he were anywhere else right now.

"Axel Johnson," Ms. Fontane says, stopping the music yet again. "That is unacceptable."

"I think it's just Lyle, Ms. Fontane," Axel replies with a grin. "He has this effect on people."

Now it's Lyle's turn to stare down at his sneakers. Unlike mine, his jeans and shoes look brand new. I imagine his mom taking him out to buy a new outfit to get him ready for the first day of school, full of hope that things will be different here.

Ms. Fontane just shakes her head. "Let's try again from the beginning."

I've made things worse for Lyle than they already were. No, we've made things worse for each other. I'm not having a future flash, but I know exactly what is going to happen. So much for flying under the radar. I have no choice. I am going to be forced to stick with Lyle. I'm going to have to protect him, to prevent him from walking into that fire, and to stop whatever happened that made him and the thing on the floor drip with blood. Thinking of that is terrible enough, but then there's the obvious questions: Will that even help? Can I stop something I've already seen in the future? I've never tried to prevent a future flash from occurring in real life because I've never seen anything so horrific before.

My stomach churns at the idea of taking on a future flash to stop it from happening. So far every single one I've had that should have come true by now has, down to the tiniest detail. Most of my future flashes have been interesting but without the threat of danger: an image of a cat that Tabitha would later adopt or the tree house Walt would build for me two years in the future. Once I saw Walt's father dying in his bed, but he was already old, with wispy white hair and crinkly yellow skin, and it didn't come as a surprise to anyone when it happened. I think of the crumb on Walt's chin this morning. *Down to the tiniest detail.* There's no way I'm going to be able to stop a fire.

On the walk back to our classroom, I hang behind the rest of the kids, avoiding everyone, especially Lyle. Laughter erupts ahead of me and I am sure that Axel is teasing him, making sure that everyone understands he's someone to avoid. I'm still digesting what I saw and need more space. I trace my finger across the door as we pass it, wishing I dared to push it open and escape into the open fields and away from school.

"Hope everyone's ready for fractions!" Mrs. Whipple announces to the class as we file back into the room. She's unaware that anything out of the ordinary has taken place in the last forty minutes and waves a handful of tests in the air as if she's handing out treats to her pet dogs.

Math has never been my subject. To be honest, aside from art, pretty much nothing has ever been my subject. But I was telling Walt the truth; I studied for this one.

Mrs. Whipple makes her way around the room, handing out the tests face down. My head reels and I can't adjust to finding myself back in the routine of a regular school day. I need to pause everything so that I can sort things out, but Mrs. Whipple has other plans.

"Alright, ready, set, go!" she says, looking up at the clock. I flip over the paper and see rows of math problems, neat and orderly. How can I focus on fractions when I'm imagining flames licking the corner of page? I peek over at Lyle, who is flipping through the pages of our math textbook. He doesn't have to take the test since it's his first day of school.

I flip my paper back over and pick up my pencil. Instead of answering whether ¾ is bigger than ⅝, I begin to sketch the scene I saw in my head. I'm always compelled to draw the images I see in my future flashes, but usually I wait until I am safely in my tree house. Today, I cover the page with flames and draw Lyle, his hair sticking up all over his head, the splatters of blood on his shirt. I squint at the image I've created. Then I remember that something or someone was lying in a pool of blood on the floor. Was it a body? Was someone else there? I shade in a spot on the floor and am so busy trying to catch the shadow exactly as I saw it, hoping that seeing it on paper will solve the mystery of who else was there, that I don't notice the real shadow over my desk as Mrs. Whipple peers over my shoulder.

"Elaine Magee!" she shrieks, tearing the test off my desk. It's barely 9 a.m. and already two teachers have reprimanded students by using their first and last names, which is never a good sign. Mrs. Whipple carries my drawing to the front of the room, holding it high in the air above her head as if it smells bad. When she reaches the trash can, she crumples it in her hand and throws it away. It's too late. The whole class, including Lyle, has already gotten a good view of the drawing.

I hate that I've done this to Lyle. While his skin under his freckles was lobster red in the gym, it is now as gray as his T-shirt. He glares at me as if I've just stabbed him in the stomach, his expression full of questions and pain.

"You don't understand," I want to say to him, but of course I don't. No one would believe the real explanation. For the second time this morning, the entire class is staring at me. I suppose, like Lyle, they think I'm just being mean. I look over at Axel and he sticks his thumb up. Considering that he's spent the last eight years targeting me, this might be considered a breakthrough. But I've never cared about Axel's approval. I gaze down at my desk and pretty much don't look up for the rest of the day, except to occasionally check the clock, whose hands appear to be stuck in one spot.

When the dismissal bell rings, I'm tempted to run home as fast as I can. My tree house is calling for me, and I want nothing more than to be propped up against my soft quilted pillow, leaning against the wood wall with a sketchbook in my hand, trying to make sense of what happened today. But when I leave the building, I see Lyle at the bike rack fumbling with his lock and I know I can't just run away. I take a deep breath and head over to the bike rack.

"Hey," I say, but he doesn't seem to hear me. I lean over the bike rack just as he pops open the lock and stands up, nearly clocking me in the chin. I jump back and Lyle looks right at me. His eyes are the same color as his freckles and they lock with mine for a moment. I realize I came over with no idea of what to say.

"Thanks for making my first day completely awful," he finally says, yanking his bike out of the rack and swinging his leg over it.

"Wait," I grab onto his handlebar before he can bike away. "I'm sorry. It's not what you think."

"Really? Then what is it? I'm dying to know." His tone indicates that he isn't.

"It's hard to explain." He looks at me, waiting. I don't have an explanation, not one that I can tell him.

"Well, when you come up with an excuse, let me know," Lyle says and then, before I can stop him, he bikes away.

So much for the new kid becoming my friend.

Chapter Four

———

THE WALK HOME TAKES LONGER THAN USUAL. I drag my feet through the dry dirt, hoping that extending the time it takes to get from school to my house will make what happened today feel farther away. The rolling hills, which have never looked like anything but rolling hills to me before, now remind me of the back of a sleeping dragon—one that could rear his fire breathing head any minute and destroy the world around it.

Tabitha is no longer on her porch when I pass by her house, but the lounging cats haven't moved since morning. They raise their heads idly and blink at me before falling back asleep. Frida surprises me by tearing past, chasing a grasshopper in the dirt. She stops and does a mid-air flip when she sees me. I pick her up and bury my face into her fur. The image of Lyle's expression after seeing the picture I drew is seared in my mind and even Frida's rumbly purr can't shake it.

"Should've just stayed with you today," I tell her. "Skipping school would've gotten me in a lot less trouble than going did." It's not that simple, of course. If I hadn't gone today, I would have to meet Lyle tomorrow. And even if I never touched his hand, that fire is still his future. The difference is that I wouldn't know about it. Maybe that's not a bad thing if I can't do anything about it anyway.

I put Frida down and shake my head, not wanting to think about any of this. She follows me as I continue toward my house. I try to shoo her back, but she's persistent and I don't have the energy to knock on Tabitha's door to return a wayward cat.

"Alright," I say, leaning down to scratch her back, "but you have to go home later." She responds by meowing and rubbing against my legs the rest of the way home.

Carmen's car is parked in front of my house. Cherry red with CARMEN'S CREATIONS painted across the side, it's hard to miss. Carmen owns a bakery and, since she closes shop at two o'clock every day, often stops by in the afternoon to keep me company until Walt gets home for dinner.

Carmen looks as unlikely to be a baker as Ms. Fontane looks to be a gym teacher. In movies, bakers are women with sweet smiles and puffs of flour on their plump cheeks. Carmen is tall and thin, all angles and candy red lipstick and matching nails. She also has a sharp sense of humor that you don't necessarily associate with a baker of cream puffs and éclairs. When I hug her hello, I can always detect a faint trace of cinnamon under her perfume.

I was four years old when I first met Carmen. I still remember Walt introducing her as his good friend. She leaned down and looked me in the eyes and shook my hand. And just like that, I had a future flash of her in a wedding dress. Her dress was a simple white sheath, paired with sparkly silver shoes. Her thick brown hair hung loose down her back.

In the future flash, Carmen waited at the end of the aisle, her arms linked with an older man who had to be her father. He was tall with the same wide smile, thick hair, and light brown skin. Chairs full of people lined the aisle—some I recognized from town and some I didn't. Carmen smiled as she began to walk down the aisle, her lips painted with the same candy red lipstick she always wears.

I opened my eyes and beamed at Carmen.

"You're gonna look like a princess at your wedding."

That was a huge compliment from four-year-old me. These days, I wear my hair short and rarely change out of my black hoodie, ripped up jeans, and shoes covered in ink doodles. But when I was four, I wouldn't leave the house unless I was wearing my pink princess dress and a tiara. I had been obsessed with Sleeping Beauty for two years.

Carmen smiled back at me. "What makes you say that?" she asked.

"I saw it. I saw you at your wedding. I closed my eyes and it was like I was there for real in the future. You were getting married and you had the prettiest dress." I sighed at the memory.

Then we both looked at Walt. A crease formed between his eyebrows.

"What do you mean it was like you were there for real in the future?" he asked.

"I saw her. I really did. She looked like a princess," I insisted. Then, to clarify, "You know how sometimes you see things that are gonna happen and then they come true?" As soon as I said it, I wasn't sure of my own words. I had experienced future flashes before, but it wasn't until I spoke about seeing Carmen's wedding that I realized I had never heard anyone else talk about seeing events from the future.

Carmen stepped back and Walt kneeled down in front of me. The color had drained from his cheeks. He grabbed my hands and pulled me close to him, his eyes level to mine. "What do you mean you see things that are going to happen? What do you mean you *saw* her? Tell me what you mean, Laney."

"I just saw her." I whispered now, sensing from Walt's tone that the answer to something important hinged on my words.

"Laney, don't say you saw something unless you really mean it. I need to know this. Did you see her at a wedding? Do you really know things are going to happen before they do?" The crease between his eyebrows deepened.

"What are you talking about? Give her a break,

Walt," Carmen said, standing up and straightening her dress. "You told me she loves princess movies. So she is having fun imagining a fancy wedding, what's wrong with that?" Walt let go of my hands, but studied my face.

"If you really saw something, tell me. You have to tell me," Walt said. "I know you can't understand, but it's very, very scary to hear—"

"I'm not expecting to get married anytime soon, Laney," Carmen interrupted. Her bright red lips trembled slightly and she ran her fingers through her hair. "But I'm glad you think I'll look like a princess when I do."

That was the first and last time I ever shared a future flash with anyone. For years all I knew was that Walt didn't like me talking about what I saw that day. It wasn't until years later that I realized Carmen was upset because she believed that even the daughter of the man she wanted to marry could see what he couldn't and still can't: she and Walt should be together.

I brought up Walt getting married to Carmen one other time. It was the afternoon of my eighth birthday and Walt headed out to buy some wood to build me a tree house just as Carmen stepped in with a bag full of groceries.

"Today I am going to teach you how to cook," she announced, setting a bulging grocery bag on the counter.

"No thanks," I said from my seat at the kitchen table. I grabbed a red pencil from my art box, carefully outlining a collar on the fuzzy puppy with floppy ears on my drawing pad. At eight, I had moved on from princesses to puppies. When begging Walt repeatedly for a puppy didn't work, I decided to cover the entire house with pictures of puppies, figuring he'd either be so moved or so annoyed that he'd give in and buy me one.

"What do you mean 'no thanks'?"

"I mean, I don't want to learn how to cook."

"But you love helping me in the bakery."

"Baking is about licking the bowl. Cooking is a means to an end." At least that's what Walt always said about cooking when he sweated over the grill or boiled our boxed macaroni noodles too long.

Carmen laughed and waved a yellow pepper in my face.

"Cooking is an art," she said. "Just like drawing puppies."

I drew swirls around my puppy's tail to indicate that it was wagging. How could Walt resist a puppy with a wagging tail? I taped my drawing on the kitchen wall next to a drawing of a puppy in a pickup truck and a watercolor of a puppy sleeping on my bed.

"Wash up in the sink," Carmen said before I could wipe my pencil-smudged palms on my jeans. As I scrubbed my hands, she dragged my chair over to the kitchen counter. When I stepped onto the chair, we were the same height.

"Why don't you see what we've got?" Carmen pushed the grocery bag toward me. I reached in and pulled out one vegetable after another until the counter was covered with eggplants, tomatoes, peppers, and onions.

"Now don't tell me this counter doesn't look like one of your pallets," she said. My eyes took in the purples, reds, yellows, and greens, and I had to admit that it did.

Carmen placed a cutting board in front of me. "Now that you're eight, you're old enough to use a knife." She handed me a knife and put an eggplant down in front of me. "But it's important to use it right. You need to hold it like this." She wrapped her hand around mine, showing me how to grip the handle. "And always cut away from yourself." Together, we sliced off the end of the eggplant. "Now you do the other end by yourself."

I cut into the other end of the eggplant and the small piece flew off the counter and rolled under the table. I put down my knife to grab the flyaway piece and throw it away, but Carmen stopped me.

"Cooking is messy, just like painting or drawing. You clean up when you're done, but you don't need to worry about it during the creative process."

"Sounds good to me."

"See? You're loving it already. Now you're going to slice the eggplant lengthwise into thin slivers." She demonstrated and I attempted to imitate her, but my piece ended up too fat at the top and too thin at the bottom. Carmen reassured me that it took time to learn and that my piece of eggplant would still taste just as good. After slicing three eggplants, we lay them on plates and salted their white flesh until drops of water appeared like dew on their surfaces. Carmen told me to blot the drops of water with a paper towel while she poured milk into one bowl and bread crumbs into another.

"Now we have to dip them in the milk and then the bread crumbs."

I dipped the first slice of eggplant in the milk and then into the breadcrumbs, accidentally knocking some crumbs out of the bowl and onto Carmen's shirt.

"Cover the eggplant, not me!" Carmen complained, but she was grinning. She reached into the bowl and sprinkled some breadcrumbs on my hair. "Now we're even."

"No way!" I laughed, tossing a pinch of breadcrumbs back at her. She threw a handful back and I ducked, turning away. That's when I noticed Walt at the door. I don't know how long he had been there, standing in the doorway like that. We had been too focused on our cooking to hear him come in. His mouth was turned up at the edges, but from the look on his face, I couldn't tell if he was holding back a smile or tears. Before I could say anything, he walked over to Carmen and me and wrapped his arms around both of us. Surprised, Carmen shrieked and then tried to push away, insisting that we were both covered in breadcrumbs and milk.

"Who cares about breadcrumbs and milk?" he said, hugging us tighter. "I love you guys."

Carmen stopped protesting and wrapped one arm around him and the other around me. I wanted to stand like that forever, smelling the cinnamon and sawdusty smells of my two favorite people.

When Carmen left that night, after the most delicious pasta dinner I'd ever eaten, Walt and I stood on the porch and watched her go. As her car pulled away, I blurted out, "Please can we keep her?" It was silly to ask like that, as if she were a puppy. I meant that I wanted Carmen to be there always.

Walt blew through his lips and cleared his throat.

"Well?" I finally asked when he didn't speak.

"I love Carmen very much, but it's complicated, Laney."

"How?"

"It's just—ever since your mother died when you were a baby—" Walt began.

My stomach tightened. Walt had told me this story before, how we were a regular happy family until my mother got pneumonia and died when I was barely a year old. I didn't know what that had to do with Carmen, but I didn't want to hear more about my imaginary mother. I squeezed my eyes shut, trying not to think about the car seat on the stoop. I didn't want to talk about how I knew that Walt was lying.

"I don't feel so good," I said, the delicious dinner that Carmen and I made souring in my stomach. "I need to lay down."

I ran to my room and flopped face down onto my bed. Walt followed me in.

"We can talk about that later if you want," he said, sitting down next to me. "You okay?"

I wanted to be angry at him, but he began rubbing my back and humming the song he always sang to me when I was little, the one about it being time for the angel to close her eyes and save her questions for another day. The next thing I knew, I was waking up to sunlight filtering in through my windows.

Fortunately for me, Carmen has stuck around.

Most days, I love coming home and telling her about my day, but I'm not in the talking mood this afternoon.

I trudge up the porch steps and open the door to find her at the kitchen table reading *Vogue* with a pile of apple donuts and two steaming mugs in front of her.

"Hi, Laney," she says, looking up from the magazine when I walk in. "Sit down and tell me everything wonderful and fabulous that happened at school today."

I snort in response and she arches her penciled eyebrow.

"That good?"

I am about to tell her that I don't want to talk about it and just want to be alone in my tree house, but the whole kitchen smells like donuts and I remember that my stomach felt like a clenched fist during lunch and I hadn't eaten a bite.

"We have a new kid in our class," I tell her, biting into a donut. It's still warm and tastes like apples and maple syrup. "And I . . ." I search for a reasonable way to explain what happened today. "I guess I . . . well, I ruined his first day."

I don't expand on this and Carmen doesn't ask; she just studies my face for a moment before leaning over to gently brush a crumb off my cheek.

"Maybe you could work on making up for that tomorrow."

"It was pretty bad. I don't think he'll want to talk to me."

"Maybe he won't talk to you, but you can talk to him. It's not like your class is that big. What's he going to do, run away every time he sees you?"

I'm tempted to tell her that's exactly what he did when I tried to talk to him this afternoon. Instead, I shrug.

We sit in silence for a bit, sipping our hot chocolate.

I look up when I hear mewing at the window. Frida is peering in, crying to come inside.

"One of Tabitha's cats," I explain to Carmen. "I might go outside and keep her company for a bit, if that's okay."

"Of course, Laney. You keep me posted on this new boy though, alright?"

"Thanks for the donuts," I say, ignoring her question. I don't want to lie to Carmen and somehow I already feel that I have.

Outside, I scoop up Frida in my left arm and use my right arm to climb up to the tree house. She makes herself at home, jumping onto my quilted pillow, walking around in two circles, and then settling in. The print of her namesake hangs above her.

"Okay, for today the pillow is yours," I tell her, leaning against the wooden wall. Walt built me this tree house four years ago when he got tired of me painting and drawing all over my room in our real house. He told me the walls in the tree house were mine and I could decorate them any way I wanted. I had seen it before in a future flash, but otherwise it looks like no other tree house I've seen—more like a mini version of our real house lifted into the sky. The sides are painted green and there are shingles on the roof. It even has glass panes on the windows so that the rain won't come in and ruin my paintings and drawings, which is a good thing because nearly every inch of the wooden walls is covered with them. Sketchbooks and piles of heavy coffee table books on various artists—Picasso, O'Keefe, Pollock—are strewn across the floor. I run my hand over the dog-eared Dali book that Walt gave me for Christmas last year and sigh. I always feel better in my tree house.

I pick up my sketchbook. On the off chance that knowing something will happen in the future gives me the power to prevent it, I might as well figure out my next steps. I decide to come up with a list of ideas for stopping Lyle from getting caught in a fire.

Nothing comes to me so I begin to sketch instead. I draw Lyle in his gray periodic table T-shirt, but in my drawing his shirt is clean. Instead of something indecipherable and bloody on the ground, I draw a wagon piled high with footballs and basketballs and baseball bats. And instead of flames licking the edges of the paper, I draw my favorite Colorado wildflower, the common Indian paintbrush. Its red pedals burst forth like flames, but safe, sweet-smelling flames.

"Much better," I say, tacking my picture onto the wall. I lean back next to Frida on the quilted pillow and study the picture in front of me. I grab my pencil and add a few more freckles to his cheeks and then study the picture again. I have to admit that I've captured Lyle perfectly. He looks as if he could step off the page. For a moment, I feel as if I *have* changed the future. I settle back into the pillow and my eyelids feel heavy. But as soon as I close my eyes, I start thinking about what I really saw. The flames, the smoke, the blood. My heart beats faster. I open my eyes and suck in the clean air around me.

It's going to take more than just drawing a picture to change the future.

Chapter Five

I SPEND THE NEXT WEEK STEERING CLEAR OF LYLE. It's not hard to do, as he has no interest in talking to me. And it's not like Ms. Fontane is going to pair us together in gym again anytime soon. No one would ever guess that I spend all day thinking about what is going to happen to the boy I'm avoiding.

On the day that Mrs. Whipple hands back our test, she pauses at my desk. While she places everyone else's tests on their desks face down, she leaves the blank sheet of paper on my desk so that the giant red zero glares up at me. I cover the zero with my hand and close my eyes. I can't stand to spend another afternoon in my tree house worrying about Lyle and the fire. As much as I don't want to, I need to face things head on. And I need to start today.

When the bell rings, I rush from our classroom and beat Lyle to his bike. He doesn't look happy to find me waiting for him.

"Hi," I say. He scowls at me and once again I'm at a loss for words.

"Leave me alone," he says.

I'm tempted to say, "I'd love to, but I've got a test with a giant red zero at the top in my backpack to remind me that I didn't make up last week's events. And by the way, you moving here has pretty much ruined my life." Instead, I scrape the toe of my shoe in the dirt. He begins to unlock his bike. I have to think of a way to stop him from biking away.

"How do you like Thornville so far?" I ask. It's not brilliant, but it's all I've got. Lyle just shakes his head and pedals away.

Soon he's nothing but a dot in the distance.

"Whatever," I say out loud. I'll try again tomorrow.

Then I notice Axel on his bike, his gaze fixed in Lyle's direction. I know that look. It's the same expression he used to get when he pulled the legs off ants.

He wasn't always mean like that. At the beginning of kindergarten, Axel and I played together almost every day. We were learning about outer space in class and at recess we pretended that the jungle gym was a rocket ship. No one else played on it because its rusty metal bars burned you on sunny days and froze your hands when it was cold. We crouched down next to each other and counted backwards to blast off. Fascinated with the idea of living without gravity, we waved our hands above our heads and pretended to grab our free-floating food from the air. Peering out from the bars, we'd tell each other what we saw passing by.

"Saturn!" I'd announce.

"A shooting star," Axel would say.

Once, Carmen flew to Mexico to visit her sick grandmother and came back with a bag of space ice cream that she bought at the airport. I brought it to school and Axel and I laughed as the sugary substance melted on our tongues. After the space ice cream ran out, Axel came to Carmen's bakery with me after school and Carmen helped us try to recreate the sweet, strawberry flavor. We ended up with a strawberry pudding that tasted good, but didn't melt in our mouths the same way.

Then that spring Axel's mom left his dad. She told him she had fallen in love with his supervisor at the chicken factory. They moved to Wyoming and she brought Axel's sister with them, leaving Axel behind. I overheard Walt telling Carmen that no one saw it coming. Axel's mom was a beautiful woman, but she spoke so quietly that you had to ask her to repeat herself every time she said something. The supervisor had a skinny neck and a pale, bald head, so different from Axel's dad with his football player build and head of thick, hay-colored hair. Walt said that Axel's dad had reacted by hitting the bottle pretty hard. My five-year-old mind pictured him setting up a bottle on a stump in his backyard and smacking it over with his hand. Now I know that hitting the bottle means smelling like stale beer and stumbling when you walk.

After his mom and sister left, Axel didn't want to play rocket ship anymore. He preferred poking a stick at an ant hole, letting the ants crawl up onto his hand. Sometimes he'd slam his hand onto the ground, squishing the ants on his palm. Then he started catching just one at a time and pinching its legs off. I couldn't stand watching those little black ant bodies wiggling in the dirt. I told him to stop and he told me to leave him alone.

A week later, someone came and removed our metal rocket ship. They did it over the weekend so when we came back to school on Monday it was just gone.

I started bringing a notebook to recess. I'd sit on the platform where the rocket ship used to be and color. Axel started calling me Art Freak and got some of the other kids to call me that too. I've stayed away from him ever since.

Now he's taking off on his bike, following Lyle.

I should call out to him to distract him, to do something. I open my mouth, then clap it shut. Do I really want to turn Axel's attention toward me?

I lean back on the bike rack and kick it with the back of my heel. I'm not having a future flash, but I'm certain that something bad is about to happen to Lyle. Why did I have to see him in that fire? Why did I have to notice that Axel is chasing after him? There's nothing I can do about any of it anyway. Maybe I should just forget about him and walk home. I kick the bike rack harder. Why did he have to move here and become *my* problem?

The few mingling students in the schoolyard continue to chat and call out their goodbyes to each other, not noticing that one of their fellow students is in imminent danger. Not that they'd even care if they knew. If you don't fit in here, you're on your own.

As much as I want to walk away, I can't leave Lyle to deal with all of this by himself. I don't know what I can do, but I need to do something. I push myself up from the bike rack and jog in Lyle and Axel's direction, slowly at first and then faster. Soon I am running, my backpack slamming against my back. Since we don't really exercise in gym class, and since I'm more likely to pick up a paintbrush than a softball bat, it only takes about two minutes for the muscles in my legs to start burning from exertion. All I can hear is the ragged bursts of my breath and the beat of my backpack. I start up a steep hill and resist the urge to stop and walk. At the top, I have to lean over to catch my breath.

Behind me, the school looks no bigger than a concrete brick. Ahead I see the two bikers on the road in the distance. Lyle, in his gray T-shirt and blue helmet, remains in front, but Axel's white head is catching up to him.

"C'mon Lyle," I say, though no one but a prairie falcon swooping down to grab a dead squirrel off the road can hear me.

Lyle holds his lead for longer than I expected. But Axel is fast. Soon he pulls up next to him.

"Pedal!" I shout. I will Lyle to move with every inch of my body.

In the distance, the two bikes collide. Then Lyle's bike tips over. Lyle flies through the air away from his bike and lands on the ground. I can tell even from the top of the hill that his body is twisted in an unnatural shape. Axel whoops as he bikes away. Lyle doesn't move.

I hesitate. When I get down there, it'll be too late to turn back. Maybe my future flash was wrong after all. As terrible as it was, I have an equally horrifying thought that I'm not sure if Lyle has a future beyond this afternoon.

I walk down the hill, hoping Lyle jumps up and bikes away before I can reach him. When I approach his bike, he still hasn't moved. I walk over until I'm standing above him, my shadow falling across his chest. Is he dead? His helmet is slightly askew and his eyes are closed. His chin is raw and bloody.

I've never seen a dead person before. A tear trickles from Lyle's closed eye down the side of his right cheek. I saw a dead deer last year in the back of a pickup truck at the gas station. Its eyes were unblinking and tear-free. Aside from the slow-moving tear, Lyle is perfectly still.

"Are you dead?" I ask him. He lets out a small snort but doesn't move.

"I wish," he says after a minute.

This seems almost worse than actually being dead so I don't reply. I take off my backpack and sit down next to him. His chin looks bad, like it could use stitches. I pull off my black hoodie and throw it on his chest.

"For your chin," I say. He holds it up to his chin without looking in my direction.

I lie back on the hard, cracked dirt. I rarely take off my hoodie and feel bare in my black T-shirt. For a while, neither of us speaks. A piece of dry grass itches my arm. I pull it out of the ground and hold it up, yellow against the bright blue sky.

Lyle reaches up to unclasp his helmet, pulls it off, and tosses it aside.

"You're lucky you had that on," I tell him.

"Right. I'm feeling really lucky today." He adjusts my now blood-soaked sweatshirt against his chin.

A car drives by and slows as it passes us. I imagine the driver peering out the window at the red-haired boy and black haired girl lying on the ground, thinking that we're just two friends taking a moment to enjoy the late September afternoon sun. The dust from the car tickles my nose, and Lyle sneezes twice.

"Why do you hate me?" he asks when he finishes sneezing. He struggles to support his weight on his elbow, winces, and then falls onto his back again.

"I don't hate you."

"I can understand why Axel hates me. There are bullies like him at every school. But I don't understand you."

It's news to me that there are kids like Axel at every school. I ponder this for a moment to avoid thinking of an answer to Lyle's question. Of course I don't hate him. I test out a few possible explanations for my actions in my head, but none of them are real. How can you lie to a boy who's laying on the side of the road with blood on his chin?

"I mean gym class was bad enough. Then you draw a picture of me all bloody and on fire? It's like you don't just hate me. You want to make sure everyone knows that you do," Lyle continues.

"I didn't mean for everyone to see that picture!" I protest.

Lyle snorts.

"Okay, I didn't even mean to draw it in the first place. It's just . . ." I take a deep breath. "Look, can you try to forget about it? Forget about the square dance and the picture and maybe we could just start over?"

"You really want me to forget that you drew a picture of me on fire? I think that image is pretty much stuck in my head."

"Yeah, it's stuck in my head too," I sigh. This can't make sense to him, but he doesn't respond.

I study the piece of grass in my hand and imagine drawing it, capturing on paper the feathery wisps that look like long eyelashes at the top. I used to draw pleasant things like flowers and pieces of grass. Now I draw things like a boy on fire. I brush the grass back and forth over the dirt next to me, watching bits of dust rise from the ground. Out of nowhere, a flash of gray tears out of the grass and pounces on my hand. A small striped cat traps the grass under her paw.

"Frida!" I cry and pick her up, scratching between her ears.

"Your cat?" Lyle asks, sneezing.

"My friend Tabitha's. I don't know what she's doing over here but I should probably bring her home."

I reach over for my backpack and stand up. Lyle looks up at me but doesn't move.

"Can you get up?" I ask him.

He pulls my sweatshirt away from his chin. The bleeding has slowed. A few drops of blood sprout on his chin, but stay in place. He hands my sweatshirt to me and I ball it up and stuff it in my backpack.

Lyle tries to push himself up with his arms and then falls back. I put Frida down and extend a hand. When he reaches up to grab it, a jolt of fear runs through me. But this time his hand is nothing but a hand and offers up no images of the future. Once he's standing, he lets go but doesn't put any pressure on his right ankle.

"We should tell someone about this, you know. You're really hurt."

"I'm okay." Lyle leans over to grab his helmet. Holding it in his hand, he limps over to his bike. He doesn't look okay and there's no debating the state of his bike. The front tire is flat and the wheel is bent. Lyle loops the strap of his helmet over his front handle-bar. "I'll admit my bike doesn't look so great." He tries to push his bike but between his limp and his bike, it looks like slow going.

"I'll push your bike," I say. "You just concentrate on walking. Hopefully you don't live too far from here?"

Lyle looks down at his foot and then his mangled bike. "I wish I lived as far away from Thornville as possible. But no, I live about five minutes away."

It takes us twenty, and by the time we are close to the dingy liver-brown ranch house at the end of the road, Lyle's face is wet with perspiration and his chin has started bleeding again, splattering dark drops of blood onto his shirt.

"Do you want my sweatshirt again?" I ask, pointing at his chin.

"Nah, I'll get something inside," Lyle says, nodding toward the house. The window shades are drawn and on such a hot and sunny afternoon the house manages to look dark. Maybe it's the thick green ivy climbing up the walls. A rusty white car is parked in front, with patches of crabgrass pushing through the cracks in the oil-stained driveway beneath it. The house, the car, and the lawn all look like they'd benefit from one of those home makeover shows Walt is always watching.

After walking down the road under the Colorado sun, which can still burn your face and neck even in September, I'm sweating too. I wait for an offer of lemonade or at least some water before I walk home.

When I don't make an effort to move, Lyle says, "Thanks," and gives me a small wave. I look at the house again, still hoping for something to drink. Then I notice the blinds in front of the house part slightly and catch a glimpse of a pale face. The face is so unexpected, like a moon in the sky at noon, and disappears so quickly that I wonder if I saw it at all. I shiver, the sweat suddenly cool on my skin.

"I'll see you tomorrow," I say to Lyle. He nods and doesn't move.

I start down the road toward my house, my throat scratchy with thirst.

When I look back, Lyle's gone.

Chapter Six

———

I'M ONLY A FEW MINUTES FROM LYLE'S HOUSE when Frida pokes her head out from the grass at the side of the road. She has clearly been following us.

"Time to take you home," I tell her. Instead, she ducks back into the grass and I follow, taking the path home through the fields. Even though I'm sweating again, I'm grateful my jeans protect my skin from the scratchy dry grass and clinging burrs. As we veer away from the road, I see nothing but golden hills and blue sky and a little gray cat darting in and out of the whispering grass.

As I walk up the first hill, a thin trail of smoke slices the blue sky in front of me. The smell of burning grass brings back the image of my future flash.

For the second time today, I run up a hill with my heart pounding, dreading what I'll see below me.

At the bottom of the hill, farther than I expected, a farmer is burning brush in his field. My eyes stay fixed on the orange glow. I'm no longer afraid of fire. I'm terrified.

When I reach Tabitha's house, I knock on the door to return Frida to her. No one answers so I walk around to the back porch.

Tabitha is watering a plant with a violet-colored watering can in one hand and talking on a plum-colored cell phone in the other.

"I'll need to find someone to watch the girls," she says into the phone. She looks up at me as I lightly rap on the side of the porch. "And I think I've found just the person to do so! I'll call you back." She hangs up the phone and smiles at me.

"How would you like to earn a little extra money?" she asks.

"Sure." I spend every penny of my allowance from Walt on pastels, drawing paper, and art books and can always use more.

"I am planning on visiting a dear friend in Wyoming next week so I need someone to watch the girls, to feed them and give them some TLC. Come in and I'll give you the key and show you what to do."

I squint at the sun lowering in the sky.

"If Carmen's home, she might be worried. I'll come by tomorrow after school," I tell her.

"Very well," Tabitha says, nodding. She's dialing the phone as I leave.

Through the screen door, I see both Carmen and Walt sitting at the kitchen table each with a mug and a pile of oatmeal cookies in front of them. Carmen taps her red nails against her mug and Walt picks at a callous on his hand. They both stop when I walk in.

"Laney!" Carmen cries. "We were getting so worried!"

"I'm sorry," I say. I check the clock. It's five o'clock. I know I'm late, but no one has ever kept track of when I get home. And it's too early for Walt to be here.

"I got a call from your teacher," he says by way of greeting. The muscle in his jaw twitches. "I heard about the drawing you did on your test."

"Was that the new boy you were talking about?" Carmen asks. "When you said you ruined his first day, is this what you meant?"

I had been dreading showing Walt the blank test with a red zero across the top, but Mrs. Whipple's call is unexpected.

"Why'd you do it, Laney?" Walt says. The crease between his eyebrows reminds me of that day all those years ago when I told him about my future flash of the wedding. *Don't say you saw something unless you really mean it. I need to know this.* I look over at our empty wood stove.

"I don't know," I say.

"Did he do something to you to make you want to do that to him?" Carmen asks. It's a reasonable question with no reasonable answer.

"Why did you draw a picture of him in a fire?" Walt says. "What made you think of that?" His voice is too loud.

"I don't know," I say again. I haven't moved from inside the doorframe. No one says anything and I listen to the clock ticking. Does it always tick this loud? Under the clock is a framed drawing of Sleeping Beauty that I drew when I was five. Her head and hands are too big, but otherwise it's a decent rendition for a five-year-old. I always felt bad for Sleeping Beauty, for how she spent her whole childhood hidden away from her parents and from the evil witch, only to prick her finger anyway. And no one even warned her about the spindle.

"Laney," Walt says, picking at the callous on his palm again, but staring straight at me. "I need to know why you drew that picture." He speaks slowly, deliberately.

I think of Walt making me promise never to go near matches. Was it more than just a request from an overprotective dad? Does he know something about what I saw? But that's ridiculous. How could he?

"I saw something on TV," I lie. "A boy in a fire. The actor looked kind of like Lyle and I wasn't really paying attention to what I was drawing. I just drew something I'd seen on TV."

Walt closes his eyes and rubs his forehead with his hand. Then he does something that surprises me. He stands up and walks over and hugs me. I breathe in his coffee and fresh sawdust smell and hug him back. I peer over his shoulder at Carmen, who looks surprised too. She flips her palms toward the ceiling and shrugs.

"Of course you're grounded," Walt says when he pulls away. "You're a talented artist, Laney, but you can't use that skill to draw pictures that will hurt other people. You need to think about your actions a little more. No television and none of Carmen's sweets for a week. You got that?"

I nod.

"I've gotta run, but I get a hug too," Carmen says. "Once you can have sweets again, I'll bring your favorite cinnamon donuts," she whispers in my ear as she kisses my cheek. Carmen leaves without saying goodbye to Walt. Maybe she's just flustered from worrying about me.

The house is quiet for a minute after she leaves. Then Walt asks me if I want to take out the Play-Doh. After all that happened today, I'd rather sit in my tree house by myself, but Walt is already grabbing a box off the shelf.

"Okay," I say as he rolls up the sleeves of his flannel and pries open a can of red.

Most twelve-year-olds have long since given up Play-Doh, but most twelve-year-olds don't live with Walt. He can make sculptures out of Play-Doh that look like they belong in a museum. He likes to joke that he's an artist like me, it's just that his only medium is Play-Doh.

"What are we making today?" he asks.

"Cats," I decide, sitting down.

"Cats?"

"I'm taking care of Tabitha's cats next week," I tell him, rolling a ball of purple Play-Doh in my hand. The cool dough feels good against my palm.

"We're going to be up all night if we're making all of Tabitha's cats," Walt laughs.

We are quiet as we sculpt. Two hours later, the table is covered in all sorts of cats—purple cats with yellow ears, red cats with blue paws, some sitting up and some sleeping with their tails wrapped around their bodies. When we both lean back to admire our work, I realize that for the past two hours, I had almost forgotten about everything that happened today. I imagine Lyle lying on the ground and worry gnaws at my stomach again.

"Are you sure everything is okay with you and that new kid—with Lyle?" Walt asks when we get up to scrub the semi-hardened dough from our fingernails. At first I'm not sure if he is talking about the picture I drew or about Axel pushing him off the bike. Then I remember that he doesn't know about Axel. I hesitate. I could tell Walt about Axel. He'll forget all about the picture I drew, but then he'll probably call Axel's dad. Lyle already thinks I hate him. Getting Walt involved in his problems will only make it worse.

"Yes," I finally say. "Everything is fine."

Walt apparently forgot about his threat of no sweets for a week because we eat Carmen's oatmeal cookies for dinner.

That night I dream about the pale face in the window.

Chapter Seven

———

THE NEXT DAY, I RUSH TO THE BIKE RACK again, beating Lyle there. This time he smiles when he approaches. I'm relieved to see he's no longer limping. And while his chin is marked an angry red, the cut has scabbed over.

"You think I actually biked here today?" he asks. "Didn't you see that thing yesterday? I'll be walking home until I can figure out how to fix that wheel." He's wearing his gray periodic table T-shirt again, though it's been washed since yesterday. The blood spots are gone. Still, I wish he would change every once in a while. The shirt makes me feel like every day could be the day of the fire.

I scan the parking lot. Axel is talking to a group of boys by the side of the school.

"Let me show you a different way home," I offer.

"A shortcut?"

"It's actually a little longer, but it's a different way than Axel goes."

Lyle looks back in their direction.

"That would probably be helpful," he says.

I lead him around the side of the school and, when we're sure no one's looking, we head out into the path toward his house. This time I'm not surprised to find Frida waiting for me in the grass.

"That cat follows you everywhere," Lyle says. I lean down to scratch her head.

"She does seem to like me," I say, pleased. "And she just reminded me that we're going to need to take a detour. I told my friend that I'd stop by to learn how to feed her cats. I'll call Carmen from there, too, and tell her that I'm going to walk you home." I'm not sure how Carmen will react to this, given that all she knows about Lyle is that I drew a picture of him on fire, but after yesterday I want to play it safe.

I point out the fork in the dirt path where Lyle should turn right to get to his house, but we continue on the same path until we reach Tabitha's.

We find her dozing on a lounge chair. She's wearing a purple floral dress, and three large cats are sleeping on her lap. Every time Tabitha lets out a snore, the cats move up and down like ships on a purple sea. Her lavender cat-eye sunglasses are pushed up into her hair, which is dangling down the side of the chair, and a fuzzy black kitten is batting at it with her paw.

"This is your friend?" Lyle whispers. Tabitha's eyes fly open.

"Laney! Who have you brought with you today?" She bolts upright and cats fly in every direction.

"When you said feed your friend's cats, you weren't kidding," Lyle whispers to me out of the corner of his mouth.

"This is Lyle," I tell her. Lyle sneezes twice into his elbow.

"Sorry," he says. "I'm allergic to cats. And pretty much everything really." He sneezes again before offering his hand. "Lyle Durand. Pleased to meet you, Ma'am."

"Oh, pshaw, none of that formality here," Tabitha says, waving him off. "You realize you're talking to a crazy old cat lady after all, don't you? You can call me Tabitha, and you don't need to bother with last names and Ma'am's and all that. Come on in kids." She opens the screen door.

I've been stopping by Tabitha's house ever since I was old enough to walk to school on my own, but continue to be a bit taken aback by the strange mix of floral perfume competing with an acidic odor every time I step into her house. In the living room, the usual multi-colored pile of cats stretches on the sofa. Everything else is a shade of purple. After years of creating art with crayons and pastels, I can name each shade—mulberry wallpaper, periwinkle rug, indigo coffee table, radiant violet bricks around the fireplace. Lyle raises his eyebrows and starts to whisper something, but I put my finger to my lips. Tabitha doesn't notice. Chatting away, she leads us into the kitchen.

"You'll need to stop by once a day to refresh their food and water," she says, deftly maneuvering through the kitchen to reach a bowl of keys on the counter. Lyle and I don't follow her. I can't imagine making my way around the kitchen as the floor is covered with ceramic cat bowls.

"Bright Purple with Ruby Red Sparkle," I say under my breath.

"Huh?" Lyle turns to me.

"I'm just trying to see how many shades of purple I recognize," I whisper. "The cat bowls are the same color as one of my crayons."

He puts his finger to his lips, imitating my earlier gesture.

Each bowl has a name written on it in dark purple paint. Daisy, Bella, Sadie, Frida . . . there are too many to count.

"Found 'em!" Tabitha says, holding up a key on a fuzzy purple chain. She notices our hesitation at the entrance of the kitchen. "Oh, you'll get used to this," she says, waving her hand at the cat bowls.

I look at the clock behind her, a magenta cat with huge eyes and a ticking tail.

"Do you mind if I call Carmen and tell her I'll be late?" I ask.

"You'll have to use my cell," Tabitha says. "No land line here." She hands me the plum-colored cell phone.

As I explain to a baffled Carmen that I'll be walking Lyle home, Tabitha continues to show Lyle what to do.

"So, I'll be home in a little bit," I say, watching Tabitha show Lyle how to unlock the door to the porch.

"The cat door is in the kitchen, but you will use this door of course. It sticks sometimes, so you really have to pull," Tabitha says, shutting the door behind her.

"Did you hear me?" Carmen asks.

"What? Oh, no, sorry,"

"When you do get home, I really need to talk to you." Her voice sounds strange, lower and quieter than usual.

"You do?"

"Yes. I have to go. I love you, Laney." The line disconnects.

"Carmen?" I hold the phone in front of me. Did Carmen hang up on me? What could she want to talk about? "I love you, Laney" rings in my ears. I know Carmen loves me but she isn't one to throw around those words lightly over the phone. And she normally ends our calls with "I'll catch you later, Laney."

"Laney, come listen to this. I need to show you where I'll hide the keys!" Tabitha calls from the porch. I try to push the phone call from my thoughts. Carmen's probably concerned after our conversation about Lyle yesterday.

Tabitha lifts up an amethyst-colored flower pot in the corner of the porch to show us where she'll hide the keys. Apparently Lyle will be helping me with the cats. I guess we're going to be friends after all.

Chapter Eight

————

WE TAKE OUR TIME ON THE PATH TO Lyle's house. There's no smoke on the horizon and if Lyle hasn't forgotten about the drawing I made, at least he doesn't mention it again.

As we cut through the cow pasture, Lyle plucks a piece of grass and presses it between his thumbs and then up to his lips. When he blows on the grass, a shrill whistle fills the air. I expect the cows around us to kick up their heels, but they continue chewing, unperturbed.

"Where'd you learn how to do that?" I ask him.

"My dad taught me. We had a field of grass behind our house in New York. Green grass, not like this dried out stuff here."

"New York?" I stop walking. "You're from New York?" I remember hoping the new kid in our class would be from New York, yet it never occurred to me to ask Lyle where he came from or why he moved to Thornville. "I've always wanted to go there, to go to the museums, to be somewhere more exciting than this dumpy old town."

Lyle sneezes. "I'm not sure you've always wanted to go to Albany. When I say New York, I don't mean New York City."

"Oh."

"But I was born in New York City," he adds as if he senses my disappointment. "My dad was in school there and my mom was an artist there for years. They moved to Albany when I was two. My dad got a job at the university teaching chemistry." He blows on the grass again. This time it sounds like a trumpet. "My dad died three years ago and we've been moving around from place to place ever since."

"How'd he die?"

"Cancer."

"I'm sorry."

We continue in silence for a while before Lyle

asks, "What about your parents?"

"What about them?"

"I mean, do you live with your mom and dad?"

"Just my dad. My mom, um, died too. Of pneumonia." I feel guilty for the lie when Lyle's dad really did die, but Walt's answer is easier than the truth. It's not like I know what happened to whoever left me on Walt's stoop all those years ago anyway. And I'm not about to talk about the car seat and the yellow note.

"It's really hard, you know?" Lyle says quietly.

"Yeah, but it's different because I was really little so I don't remember anything about her." To avoid further questions about my family, I quickly ask, "Is your mom still an artist? I'd like to see her stuff." I don't know anyone in Thornville who would call herself an artist. The closest thing we have to art in Thornville is one of Carmen's pastries. Not that her pastries aren't fabulous, but I'd love to meet someone who could teach me how to paint better, someone who would appreciate talking about different art I've admired in books.

"She draws stuff for medical textbooks to make money, but she's given up painting the way she used to do it."

I think of the pale face behind the blinds.

"Maybe she'd start up again?"

"No," Lyle says. He doesn't explain beyond that and I sense that I shouldn't ask.

"Thanks for showing me a different walk home," Lyle says as we get near his house. "Might keep me alive for a while longer."

"What?" I nearly choke on the word. The image of fire flashes before my eyes.

"I'm just joking. I don't think Axel will actually kill me, but at least this way I can get to school and back without any broken bones." He spits out the last words. I look at the scab on his chin.

"Oh," I say. "I wasn't thinking about that."

Lyle snorts. "What were you thinking? Is there some other threat to my life I don't know about?"

"No, no. I mean, no, of course not," I stutter. I'm not about to try to explain that I can see the future. "But you need to tell someone about what Axel did. You should tell your mom, or tell Mrs. Whipple or something. It's not right."

"It doesn't help to tell people stuff like this. It only makes it worse," Lyle replies.

That sounds wrong to me, but I've made my own choices about secrets, so I don't argue.

Chapter Nine

————

WHEN I GET HOME, CARMEN IS SITTING at the kitchen table with a spread in front of her that looks fit for a banquet: three plates piled high with cinnamon donuts, oatmeal cookies, and banana chocolate chip muffins.

"Are we having a party?" I ask, sitting down and grabbing a muffin.

"No, I just wanted to make something nice for you," Carmen says. She smiles at me, but her smile wavers. I put the muffin down.

"Just because?"

"I have to tell you something, Laney," she says, twisting a strand of hair with her finger.

"Okay."

"I'm leaving—" she begins, but her voice quivers.

Her eyes fill with tears and she wipes them with the back of her hand, leaving a dark streak of mascara across her cheek.

"You're leaving? Where are you going?" I try to imagine my life without Carmen in it. I think about coming home to an empty house every day, a house that's too quiet without her laughter filling it. "You can't leave Thornville."

"Oh, Laney, I'm not really going anywhere. I'm leaving Walt." His name comes out as more of a sob than a word. She wipes another streak across her cheek. For a moment I'm so distracted by the black marks on Carmen's normally perfect face that I can't process her words. I hand her a napkin and she dabs at her eyes.

"Does he know?"

"Yes, yes. I told him today."

I don't ask why. I know why. But Carmen tells me anyway.

"Remember when you were little and you said you saw me at my wedding? You were always such a sweet little girl, Laney. You still are." She presses the napkin against her eyes and holds it there for a moment. "I want a wedding, Laney. Not just the wedding, I mean, but I want to get married, to live with you and your dad, to be a real family. Walt isn't ready for that and I'm starting to realize that maybe he never will be."

I look down at my hand and see that I've flattened the muffin under it. Crumbs scatter across the table.

"He's not my dad," I say, angry now. I clap my hand over my mouth. I've never told anyone that I know Walt isn't my father. As upset as I am, I'm not ready to lose him.

"Oh, Laney, of course he's your dad. Don't say that," Carmen says. I chew on a fingernail, relieved she didn't take my outburst literally. "I know you might be mad at him—"

"What I mean is, it's not right. It's not fair to you or to me!"

"I know that he loves me, Laney, and he's a good man. He has his reasons, but I just can't—" She begins to cry again, unable to finish.

I wipe my muffin-smeared hand on my jeans. Then I pull my chair next to hers and lean my head against her shoulder. She leans her head on mine, her soft, chestnut brown hair falling over my face. She smells, as always, like perfume and cinnamon.

"I'll still come see you sometimes, Laney. I talked to Walt about that already. I just won't, you know, stay for dinner, or come over on the weekends or stuff like that. And for the next few weeks, I probably won't come over as often in the afternoons because it'll be hard for me to be here."

"What are his reasons?" I ask her. "You said he has his reasons. What are they?"

She pulls away and looks at me.

"You know about Aster, Laney. He's never really gotten over her."

Aster is the name that Walt gave to my imaginary mother. I've never talked to Carmen about her, but apparently Walt told her the same story. Then I realize that maybe there really was an Aster and Walt really did love her. Maybe they even dreamed of having children together and then she died before they could.

"So, he loved her? And that's why he can't marry you?"

Carmen looks away. "Maybe you should ask Walt more about her. He doesn't like to talk about it, but it's only fair that you know about your mom."

My stomach clenches. Walt told Carmen the same lie. She doesn't know about the car seat or the yellow note.

The door opens and Carmen and I both look up. Walt is standing in the doorway. He looks like he's aged ten years since I kissed him goodbye this morning. His bloodshot eyes glow like hot coals and his mouth is twisted unnaturally.

"I'm gonna get going," Carmen whispers to me. She kisses my cheek before she goes. Walt steps back to let her pass.

"I'm sorry, Laney," he says in a strangled voice. The door bangs as Carmen walks out.

"You should be!" I shout. I follow Carmen out. My stomach tightens as I climb the rungs of my tree house. I never argue with Walt. He's always been good to me and I've never wanted to give him reason to regret bringing me in from that cold stoop. He took me when I was alone in the world and I'll never forget that. It's just that I don't think I can stand to be in the same room with him tonight.

Chapter Ten

———

AFTER SCHOOL THE NEXT DAY, I'M SURPRISED to find Lyle already waiting for me at the bike rack.

"Still no bike," he says, "But I thought you'd be here. I have something I want to show you."

"What is it?"

"You'll have to wait until you come to my house, but I think you'll want to see it."

"Can you give me a hint?"

"Nope."

This time Lyle leads the way down the dirt path. I'm happy to have an excuse not to go home to an empty house.

"You changed your shirt," I blurt out with relief as I read GOT SCIENCE? on the back of his navy blue

T-shirt. Somehow I hadn't noticed in class today.

"What?"

My face burns red. It wasn't a nice thing to say.

"Nothing," I tell him.

It's a rare cloudy day for late September in Colorado. I breathe in the smell of fall as we walk—hay and dust with a twinge of cow manure. Behind us the school and the beige strip of stores that make up Thornville grow smaller. Ahead of us is nothing but rolling hills, a handful of trees, and scattered houses and farms. We take our time and don't say much. I pluck pieces of grass as we go and chew on one of them, watching the feathery top of it bob up and down with each step.

"Teach me how to make that sound you made with the grass."

Lyle plucks a piece of grass and places it upright between his two thumbs, cupping his other fingers around it.

"Hold it like this," he says, extending his arms so that I can see the position of his hands. I pick a new piece and place it between my thumbs. "Now it's simple. Just blow."

I blow between my thumbs as hard as I can. It sounds like a fart. Lyle laughs until he starts sneezing again.

"Adjust the grass a little so that it's tight between your fingers. Then blow." He demonstrates and makes another piercing sound.

As we walk up the hill, I attempt again with no luck.

"I can't do it."

"Clearly," he says, laughing harder.

"Ha, ha," I reply. Lyle begins to say something back, but I hold up my hand for him to stop. I hear voices but don't see anyone.

"Who is that?" a voice calls from over the hill.

My eyes meet Lyle's. We stop walking.

"Who's up there?" someone yells again and I recognize the voice.

I hold a hand up to prevent Lyle from answering, but I can tell by his face that he knows Axel's voice too.

We don't move.

A cloud passing overhead casts a shadow across the hill. The voices on the other side start up again, hopefully having forgotten about us. I'm about to whisper to Lyle that we should turn around and walk the other way when I get a whiff of something sharp and unpleasant. It smells like smoke but has a chemical tinge to it. I remember the farmer burning hay in his yard yesterday and look around but see no sign of smoke.

"Let's go," Lyle whispers.

"Hold on a minute." I crouch down and begin to climb the rest of the hill in a crawl. I look back at Lyle, who raises his eyebrows and shakes his head. I feel foolish, like a little kid playing a silly spy game, especially since the smell has disappeared with the breeze, but I need to see what's over the hill.

When I near the top, I look over my shoulder. Lyle still hasn't moved. I continue to crawl and nearly cry out when my shin bangs against a rock. I pull myself up to a crouch, rubbing my shin, and peer down below me. Axel and two other boys are huddled together. An instant later they break their huddle and throw something into the air. It's a small object and it glows white-blue. It lands in the dry creek bed next to them and Axel stomps it out with his foot.

"Awesome!" one of the boys yells.

"Let's do another," Axel says, pulling something from a box. My heart pounds so hard in my chest it might burst right out and land on the cracked dirt in front of me, but I creep down a little farther.

A small box next to them reads GI JOE ACTION FIG-URES in silver letters across the side. Axel lights another one of the green plastic figures on fire. I smell the smoky chemical odor again.

We are surrounded by dry fields. I can't remember the last time it rained. A spark could set everything ablaze. There's more than just the fear of the fire from my future flash gnawing inside of me. A lifetime of warnings about fire pumps through my veins and my heart races faster.

Something rustles behind me. Then Lyle's arm brushes against mine. He wrinkles his nose at the smell. I worry that he'll sneeze but he doesn't make a noise.

Axel stomps on the second burning GI Joe. He inspects the bottom of his shoe.

"Nice one," he says, pulling another out. My mouth feels like it's full of dry dirt. When I try to swallow I make such a loud gagging sound that I'm sure they hear me. I hold my breath.

"Let's do another," Axel says, and I exhale.

Lyle motions for me to turn around.

Can I leave knowing that they could start a fire any minute? Does the fire I saw begin now, with these burning toys? Does Lyle run into a nearby house before the fire swallows the whole field and all of us in it?

Then I remember his shirt. Blue. Today is not the day.

I begin to follow Lyle back up the hill when something changes. It takes me a minute to figure out what it is. I no longer hear voices below me. A prairie falcon flies above me and I wonder if it's the same bird I saw yesterday. This thought is running through my head when I turn around and see all three boys staring up at us.

Chapter Eleven

R UN!" I YELL TO LYLE. WE SCRAMBLE TO THE top of the hill and fly down the other side.

My legs feel as flimsy as pieces of grass, bending and wobbling beneath me. Ahead, Lyle loses his balance. His knee hits the ground but he pushes himself back up and manages to keep running.

"Losers!" Axel shouts from behind us. I don't look back. I can't tell if he is two feet or a mile away. I run. The air stings my lungs.

"Losers!" I hear again, closer this time. I stumble along the path behind Lyle, focusing on the back of his T-shirt. I know it's only a matter of time before Axel's hard grip on my shoulders yanks me back. Instead, I feel a hard pellet of water hit my arm and then my face. A second later, the cloud above us unleashes the unexpected. Rain. The sound is deafening as water slams into the hard earth and thunder groans from above. The rain comes in all directions, pouring from the sky and bouncing back from the earth in protest. It soaks my hair, my skin, my clothes. I slip on the wet ground and pull myself up, determined to keep up with Lyle. For a skinny, sneezy boy who recently injured his ankle, he has surprising speed. My sneakers and jeans feel like weights covered in heavy mud and grass, but I keep running.

We are nearly to Lyle's house when the rain ends as suddenly as it began. Lyle peers quickly over his shoulder as he runs and then skids to a stop on the slick path. I almost bump into him before I stop myself. He stands still and scans the horizon.

"They're gone," he gasps. I whirl around and see nothing but glistening golden grass and a freshly scrubbed blue sky, with the dark cloud retreating over the hill. I bend over to catch my breath. My shoes are brown globs and my jeans are soaked.

We both stand there, sucking in air and watching the hill. I wait for Lyle's accusation. I wait for him to ask me why I had to do it, why I had to go farther down the hill, why I had to risk them seeing us like that. I'm already rehearsing my answer. *You didn't have to follow me. And anyway, it's your fault. I would never have gone closer if I wasn't trying to protect you.*

"So, do you want to see it?" Lyle asks when he can speak again.

"See what?"

"The whole reason you are over here! I wanted to show you something, remember?"

I had forgotten.

I wipe a strand of wet hair from my face.

"But what about—" I cut myself off. Why am I bringing up something I did wrong if Lyle's not going to? "Okay. Sure, let's see it."

Lyle looks over at my muddy clothes. "Just don't touch anything, okay?"

"Touch what? I don't even know what you're talking about." I still feel defensive, but Lyle doesn't mention anything about Axel or burning GI Joes.

My feet slosh in my shoes as I follow Lyle to the house. I expect him to go in, but he passes the front door and continues toward the side. I am cold, the wet clothes clinging to my body causing goose bumps to sprout on my arms.

Lyle lifts a rusty latch on a wooden gate and the battered door swings open. His backyard is not faring much better than the front—a patch of scrubby crab-grass struggling to survive in hard dirt. The blinds are drawn on the windows in the back of the house as well, and a cool breeze ruffles the ivy that creeps along the side of them. Does a white hand separate the blinds and press quickly against the glass? Or did I imagine that? I rub my arms to keep warm.

Lyle heads toward a building in the corner of the yard. It's not large enough to be called a house, but it's larger than most sheds I've seen. With the same chipped liver-brown paint, it must have been built at the same time as the house. A padlock hangs from the door. Lyle pulls a keychain out of his pocket. He looks over his shoulder past me before using one of the keys to open the lock. I turn around too, but the blinds remain still this time.

"C'mon," he whispers.

"Why are we whispering?"

Lyle motions for me to step into the building. "I

don't know if my mom would want us in here," he says, shutting the door behind me. It's instantly so dark that I can't see my hand in front of me. I blink several times but nothing changes. I reach out to establish my balance but then remember Lyle telling me not to touch anything.

"Lyle?"

"Sorry. I've just gotta find the light. It's on a chain in here somewhere." He bumps around the room. Something smells familiar. I recognize it before Lyle turns on the light. Dried paint and turpentine. When the light fills the room, we are surrounded by canvases and art supplies.

My eyes widen at the room before me. A canvas larger than I am is propped against the wall. The canvas is painted black with orange, yellow, and hot pink streaks shooting across it. The streaks on the canvas look alive. It's like nothing I've seen before.

"It's wonderful," I say, shaking my head.

I take another step into the room and absorb all of the artwork around me. Most of the paintings are abstract, bold swatches of color jumping off the canvases. A few of them toward the back are more representative, images of women with big hair and dark eyes set against vivid backgrounds.

I love all of it and want to breathe it in at one time. Goosebumps pop up on my arms again, but this time not because I'm cold.

"This must be what it's like to go to an art museum," I murmur.

"Not quite," Lyle replies. I jump at the sound of his voice, having forgotten he was even in the room with me. "Museums aren't this messy."

It's true that there isn't a lot of order to the room. There are wooden shelves along the walls, but the canvases look like they were shoved into them without much thought and some of the paintings have fallen onto the floor, face down. Making my way toward the back of the room, I nearly trip over a black metal art box. The box is tipped on its side with paint tubes and brushes strewn across the floor in front of it. Despite Lyle's warning not to touch anything, I lean down to clean up the art supplies. The tubes of paint feel like rocks, hardened all the way through.

"Your mom is an amazing artist. She really doesn't paint anymore?" I ask Lyle as I shut the art box. He bites his lip and shakes his head.

Then I notice something in the corner of the room. It's a small canvas, the size of a magazine, and it's partly obstructed by another painting in front of it. The style of the painting looks different from anything else in the room, darker and more precise. I walk over to it, stepping over fallen canvases. It takes some effort to move the canvas in front of it, as it's blocked by a large can of turpentine. When I manage to pull the painting out, I nearly drop it.

It's a painting of a black-haired baby in a car seat, sitting on an icy, cracked front stoop. It's a painting of me.

Chapter Twelve

L ANEY? LANEY? ARE YOU OKAY?" I CAN HEAR Lyle's voice. It has an echoing dreamlike quality, like he's talking through a long tube. The whole world has shifted in an instant. Lyle and the rows of canvases have become a whirl of bright colors surrounding the only thing I can focus on. The painting of me. It has to be me. The pink blanket, the black swirl of hair, the cheeks rosy in the cold night air.

And yet it's impossible. What would a painting of me be doing in Lyle's mom's art shed? How could there be a painting of a moment that only Walt and I know about? Walt and I and one other person, the person who dropped me off.

I pick up the painting and clutch onto it with both hands.

"I need to talk to your mom," I say to Lyle, my eyes not leaving the painting.

"What? Why? No, you can't talk to her!"

"You don't understand. I need to."

"Laney, I should never have showed you all this. I did this as a favor to you. You can't—"

I push past him and through the art shed. Once again I stumble over the art box, tipping it over and spilling the paint tubes across the floor.

When I open the door, the glare of the outdoor light is momentarily blinding.

"Laney, stop!" Lyle calls from behind me.

I squint into the intense sunlight and run toward his house, the painting pressed against my chest. I run up the porch steps and to the back door, hesitating for only a second before pounding on it with my fist.

"Laney," Lyle says, running up the steps behind me. "What are you doing?"

I keep knocking on the door.

"She won't answer, you know," Lyle says. His voice is quiet. I stop knocking.

"Why? Why won't she answer?"

"She won't talk to anyone, it's not just you. She's been like that since my dad died." His voice is still quiet. I can see him in the reflection of the glass in the door, standing there on his back porch, scrawny and wet, blinking. I should drop the painting or say something comforting to Lyle, but the urgency of understanding why I found a painting of me in Lyle's shed shoves away my other thoughts.

"I need to talk to her, Lyle. It's really important."

"What's so important about that painting? You freaked out when you saw it."

"It's me. It's a painting of me." I continue to clutch the painting, but face it toward him so he can see. He looks at me, then the painting, then back again.

"It does kind of look like you—"

"That's because it *is* me!"

"I mean, you have the same gray eyes and black hair. But Laney, it mostly just looks like a painting of a baby. It could be anyone. I mean, anytime anyone knows someone else with red hair, they tell me I look just like him. Do you know how many times people have told me I could be twins with Ron Weasley in *Harry Potter*?"

"What? No, Lyle, it's not like that."

I'm not about to explain about the car seat and the stoop so I turn around and ignore him and bang on the door again.

"Mrs. Bertrand! Could I come in?"

The house remains silent. The only sound is the clatter of Lyle's teeth as he shivers.

"I think you should go home, Laney," he says. "I should never have shown you those paintings."

I drop my hand to my side, studying the blinds one last time. Nothing.

"I really want to talk to your mom."

He attempts a smile. I think he feels bad for me. The crazy girl who thinks she's in a painting.

"You should go."

"Okay," I say, not moving.

Lyle's shaking harder now and will probably get sick because I've kept him on the porch so long.

"Really, Laney. Go home."

I take one last look at the door.

"I'm sorry Lyle."

"Go."

I walk past him, off the porch and across the yard.

I glance once in the direction of the shed. The door is still open. I can see the burst of color inside. No one would guess from the outside of that dingy looking shed that it could contain so much brightness or such an important secret. I pass through the gate, across Lyle's front yard, and up the path. I nearly slip twice on the muddy ground. The whole time, I never let go of the painting.

When I get home, I quickly cut around the back to my tree house. I want Walt to see me with the painting about as much as I'd want him to see me with a lighted match. Climbing to the tree house, with one arm on the ladder and one holding the painting, reminds me of the day he taught me how to use a hammer. I busted my thumb three times helping him nail the rungs to the tree, but we both laughed when I scrambled to the top the first time, pleased with our construction. That day seems like it happened in another lifetime after all that's happened over the past week. I leave the painting in the corner of the tree house, facing the wall. I'm angry at Walt, but I'm not ready to tell him that I know he's not my father.

Chapter Thirteen

———

I'M NOT SURPRISED WHEN LYLE DOESN'T SHOW up for school the next day. I feel a twinge of guilt when I look at his empty chair in the morning. I got him chased and then kept him cold and wet on his back porch. But I'm full of so many emotions these days that the feeling of guilt is like one more splatter of paint on a Jackson Pollock painting. I don't think about it, or him, for the rest of the school day.

I do think about him when I stop by Tabitha's on the way home from school. I find the key under the flower pot on the back porch, but when I stick it in the back door's keyhole and pull on the knob, nothing happens. The cats' meows from inside grow louder each time I rattle the door. Even Frida looks disappointed, eyeing me from her perch on the porch rail. It's not until I'm about to give up that I remember Tabitha explaining to Lyle that the door doesn't always open easily. I shake the handle again and push against the door. After several more attempts, it gives with a low moan.

"Sorry, kitties. I thought that Lyle was listening to the directions so I didn't need to," I explain from the doorway to the pile of cats on the couch. They're not interested in my excuses. The whole chorus of them follows me into the kitchen, mewing plaintively at my legs until I find the alizaram crimson bin full of food.

Filling their water bowls is no easy task either. It's challenging enough to walk through a maze of cat bowls without the floor being slick with water. The cats don't appreciate the water on the floor and continue to mew, lifting their front feet and shaking them dry in disgust. The bowls are heavier than I would've expected and it isn't until my arm begins to ache that it occurs to me to use one of her watering cans instead of picking up each bowl.

When I finish my cat feeding duty, I sit on the porch for a while. Frida pokes her head out of the cat door and then joins me by curling up on my lap.

Warm and purring, she's nice company, but I have to admit that I miss Lyle. Despite all of the stress that he has caused me, I've gotten used to having him around. It wouldn't just be easier at Tabitha's if he were with me—it'd be more fun.

At home, I climb up to the tree house and study the painting again. I have very few pictures of myself as a baby. Walt never thought to take any, so the only pictures are ones that Carmen took on outings with Walt and me. The image in my mind from the night Walt found me is clearer than any photograph, but only from my perspective. I couldn't see my own gray eyes staring up at Walt, or at whoever left me there. I look at the baby in the painting. Lyle thought it could be anyone. How many gray-eyed, black-haired babies are left on a stoop in the cold? I trace my hand over the baby's pink blanket and then notice the word LAZOS written in small black print in the bottom right corner of the painting. I don't know how I missed it before. Who is Lazos? And why did Lyle's mom have this painting? The questions repeat themselves in my head like a riddle, but I find no answer.

At dinner, Walt pushes his pasta around his plate and doesn't eat. He looks so sad that I can feel the ball of anger at him crumbling inside of me.

"I love you, Laney," he says when I finish eating. I put my hand out and he covers it with his own. Questions about the painting and that night on the stoop clog my throat, but I bite my lip and swallow them down. Then I clear the dishes and go to my room to do some homework. When I turn out the light, Walt's still sitting at the kitchen table with his untouched food.

The next day, Lyle's seat is empty again. I find myself peeking over at it all morning, as if Lyle might suddenly appear. He must be pretty sick to miss another day of school. I don't have his phone number so calling to check on him is out. I'd have to stop by his house. I imagine knocking on the door of his house again, only this time Lyle answers it. He's healthy enough, just a bad runny nose and maybe sneezing a little more than usual. His mom is standing behind him and, seeing me, changes her mind about avoiding other people. She urges me to come in, saying she has something she needs to tell me. Something about a painting in her shed.

I'm imagining this turn of events when Mrs. Whipple interrupts my thoughts: "Aren't you going to join the class, Laney?"

All of the desks around me are empty.

"They've gone to gym," she says, shuffling through papers on her desk as she talks. "You should join them."

I nod and stand up.

"Oh, and Laney?" she says as I'm walking to the door. "Take it easy on the new kid, okay? He doesn't need kids teasing him. In fact, he could probably use a friend."

Trust me, I get it, I think. "Okay," is all I say.

I run my hand along the wall in the hall, taking my time to get to the gym. I pause when I pass the school's front door. My fantasy about my conversation with Lyle and his mom felt so real that it almost seems possible. Maybe I will run out the door and keep going until I reach Lyle's scrubby lawn.

Instead, I keep walking until I hear Ms. Fontane's

voice. She's explaining the waltz, something she's been trying to teach us since first grade. In six years, none of it has stuck. The only thing I know about the waltz is that it means sweaty palms and squashed toes. I push open the gym door just in time to be assigned my dancing partner. Axel.

He smiles at me when Ms. Fontane calls our names. For some reason he's going to enjoy this, though I can't imagine why.

"Hi, Art Freak," he says, walking toward me. I roll my eyes and don't reply.

"Aren't you going to say hello?" he asks, his breath hot on my face. He smells like Doritos and body odor. It's not a pleasant combination but I resist the urge to comment, knowing that I already pressed my luck on the hill the other day.

"Are you going to freak out when we start dancing or do you only do that with your boyfriend?" he asks, grabbing my hands. I tense for a moment and am relieved when no future flash comes to me.

Axel's grip is too hard, though. I wiggle my hands, but he holds on tight.

"He's not my boyfriend."

"Sure looks like it to me."

"Shut up, Axel."

"Well, how sweet. You two even sound alike," Axel sneers.

"What are you talking about?"

"Shut up, Axel," he imitates, only in a high-pitched voice that sounds nothing like me or Lyle. "That's what Lyle said to me the other day, too." He sniggers and I breathe in another blast of Dorito breath.

My stomach clenches.

"What other day?"

Ms. Fontane interrupts us. "Axel and Laney, three steps. Left, right, left." She watches as Axel and I make a feeble attempt to follow her instructions. Axel steps on my foot twice and then pushes us both back so that we bump into another set of dancing partners.

"Move back, Axel and Laney. And smoother, you need to work together." Ms. Fontane says, her right hand tapping out some sort of beat on her left hand, though it has nothing to do with the music.

"What other day?" I hiss when she turns around to focus on another inept pair of dancers.

"The other day when Lyle and I were hanging out."

"Left, right, left!" Ms. Fontane yells to the class.

"When were you and Lyle hanging out?"

"Oh, we're good friends. We hang out all the time," Axel says, smiling again. Parts of his teeth are coated with an artificial orange film. "Why do you look so concerned? Let me guess. You're jealous. You don't like the idea of your boyfriend having other friends."

I picture Lyle on the ground next to his bike, blood on his chin and a trickle of water running down his cheek.

"What did you do to him, Axel?"

His jeering tone lowers to an angry whisper. "Nothing that little spying punk didn't deserve. And come to think of it, he wasn't by himself on the hill that day, was he? You better watch yourself Laney."

"You—you better watch yourself too, Axel," I tell him. It makes no sense coming out of my mouth. Axel stands over a head taller than me and the lack of blood in both my hands at the moment is a blatant reminder of his strength.

He laughs, another blast in my face.

"I'm really scared, Laney. Really, really scared."

"Left, right, left!" Ms. Fontane yells again.

I look down at my feet so I won't have to look at Axel's face. His Dorito breath is making me nauseous. I concentrate on our shoes, my cat-covered Converses and his black high-top sneakers, clumsily moving back and forth. Axel intentionally stomps on my right foot. His shoe leaves a dirty smudge over my drawings.

"Everyone against the wall! You are all still bumping into each other. Ava and Jack will show you all how it's done!" Ms. Fontane yells, pulling aside one of the couples. I gladly let go of Axel's hand and walk over to the wall with his words echoing in my head. *Nothing that little spying punk didn't deserve.* How did he get to Lyle if Lyle's been home sick for the past two days? If Lyle's mom wouldn't open the door for me, there's no way she'd let in the school bully. Maybe nothing happened. Maybe Axel is doing nothing more than trying to scare me. Unfortunately, it's working. My earlier daydream of Lyle opening the door of his house for me has been shattered, replaced with the image of him lying bloody on the ground.

The rest of the day creeps by. Once again, the clock's hands seem to be stuck in one place. Only when I look at them today, I feel a combination of relief and frustration. I dread going to Lyle's, but I need to know if anything happened. I can't bear to wait until Monday to find out.

When the last bell rings, I resist the urge to run outside. I wait to gather my books and fill my backpack, giving Axel plenty of time to head out a good distance ahead of me. By the time I leave the building, no one is in the school yard except for the small gray-and-white cat waiting for me.

"We've got a job to do before I feed you," I tell Frida and then jog down the road, taking the quickest route to Lyle's. It's a windy afternoon, the air colder than it's been this fall. It must be a downslope wind, blowing the cold air from the Rocky Mountains into town. I lean against the wind and have to jog backwards from time to time to avoid dirt blowing into my eyes.

The first thing I notice at Lyle's house is his bike, lying on its side on the lawn. It was probably propped up against the side of the house but then blown over by the wind. The tire has been fixed.

I walk to the front door, not daring to pause to

think about what I'm doing, and knock lightly, nothing like the way I banged on the back door the other day. I can hear a car in the distance and the wind slamming a door open and closed somewhere. The house is quiet.

"Lyle!" I yell, knocking on the door harder. Frida meows from the bottom of the steps, reminding me that I should be at Tabitha's feeding the cats. I knock a few more times. They have to be home. His mom's car is parked in the driveway and with his bike here, Lyle can't have gone far. I try the doorknob but it's locked.

I sit on the stoop and wait. I've been waiting all day. Waiting for the clock at school to strike three, and now waiting on Lyle's front stoop. I wrap my arms around my body, cold in my cotton hoodie. It's not my usual sweatshirt, but another black one. My favorite sweatshirt is now in a ball in the back of my closet. Even though it's clean, I can't wear it without thinking of Lyle's bloody chin.

"It's cold out here!" I yell to the house. No answer.

I arrived determined to wait on the stoop for as long as it took for someone to open the door, but after five minutes I give up. If Lyle's home, he's not budging.

Chapter Fourteen

WHEN I GET HOME, I INSTINCTIVELY look for Carmen's car. I need to stop doing that. Instead, I see Walt's blue pickup truck parked in the driveway. He's home early. I scan over the events of the day in my mind, but there's nothing Mrs. Whipple could have called him about today.

When I open the door, Walt is at the table again, this time with a yellow sheet of paper in his hands. I freeze at the doorway.

"Laney," he says, quickly folding the paper and shoving it in his pocket. "Come sit down."

I scan the room. Did he find the painting? Are we going to discuss that night? The yellow paper? The car seat on the stoop?

"You look like I'm going to bite you or something!" He pats the seat next to him.

"You're home early," I say, sitting down reluctantly.

"I know. It's just the past couple of days . . . Look, I'm a little bit worried about you is all."

"Me? You're worried about me?" I glance at the thick stubble on his cheeks and darkening circles under his eyes.

"Yeah, I know, I'm not doing so great myself. But this is about something else. You'll think this is ridiculous, but I need to ask you again about that drawing . . . You said you drew it because of a television show you saw. Is that really why?"

"Did Mrs. Whipple call you again or something?"

"No, it's not that. I've just been thinking about it. I want to understand why you did that, Laney." He puts his hand on top of mine, his eyes searching my face.

"What were you reading when I came in?" My voice sounds too high pitched to be my own, almost disconnected from me somehow.

"Huh?"

"That yellow sheet of paper. What was that?" I've taken a leap off a diving board. My stomach reels trying to catch up with the move I just made.

The muscle twitches in Walt's jaw. "That paper? That was nothing."

"The picture was nothing either," I reply. Walt looks hurt but at the moment I don't care. "I made a mistake, that's all. And by the way, you should know about making mistakes!"

"I'm not just asking to bother you, Laney. I—"

"Then don't ask. Can I go out to the tree house now?"

Walt nods, gazing down at his hands. I slam the door on the way out and climb up the tree house ladder. The painting is still there, exactly where I left it.

My heart is thudding in my chest. The yellow paper. Walt still has the yellow paper. I look at the painting and realize that the yellow sheet of paper on the stoop next to me is the only thing missing to make the painting of that long ago evening complete.

Chapter Fifteen

———

THE WEEKEND DRAGS BY. WALT SPENDS MOST of it slumped on the couch in front of the television watching football and home improvement shows, and I spend most of it in my tree house, flipping through art books and drawing pictures of Frida curled up on my pillow, wishing my thoughts weren't so jumbled in my head. On Sunday, I'm tempted to try knocking on Lyle's door again, but decide it's pointless.

When Monday finally arrives, I'm relieved to see Lyle in his seat as I walk into the classroom. He's facing away from me, staring out the window. I resist the urge to run over to him. I want to yell at him for not letting me in his house but also to make sure that he's okay. I need to know that Axel was lying about running into him.

When I reach my seat, I intentionally let my backpack slam against the desktop. Lyle turns toward me. Axel was telling the truth.

Lyle's right eye is nearly swollen shut. The lid is shiny and purple. The scab on his chin has been opened again and is patched with a blood-soaked gauze pad and tape. He stares at me for a second with his good eye and then looks away before I can say anything.

I glance over at Axel. He flashes me a huge grin. The classroom has taken on a dream-like quality and I feel as if I could float away if I don't hold onto something tightly. I grip the sides of my desk to steady myself.

"Good morning, class!" Mrs. Whipple calls from the front of the classroom. "Have a seat please, Laney." I sink down into my chair. I need to tell someone about Lyle. But first, I need to talk to him. Recess. I can talk to him at recess. Once again I find myself staring at the classroom clock.

Mrs. Whipple opens her attendance book and begins to call out names, even though she could easily glance around the classroom and see that all thirteen seats are filled, avoiding the process entirely.

When she gets to Lyle, she looks up and then pauses.

"Lyle, what happened to your eye?"

The entire class turns in his direction.

"My bike," he mumbles. "I fell off my bike again." The skin under his freckles burns red. He sneezes twice, wincing after each one.

"Well goodness, try to be more careful!" Mrs. Whipple studies him for a moment longer and then continues down the list.

The morning drags. My constant glances at the clock catch Mrs. Whipple's attention.

"Laney, is there somewhere else you'd rather be today?"

Anywhere. I'd like to be anywhere else. I don't respond.

I think about Salvador Dali's paintings of melting clocks and imagine our classroom clock sliding down the wall and into a puddle on the floor. It could happen. Nothing feels real today.

At eleven o'clock, the recess bell finally rings. I

decide to wait to approach Lyle until everyone is outside. I find him leaning against the school building,
hugging his knees.

"Hey," I say, sitting next to him on the asphalt.

"Go away, Laney."

I wasn't expecting that. I blink back tears.

"Are you mad at me about the painting? Because
I'm sorry about that. I know I acted crazy. If you knew
why, you'd understand, I promise, but—"

"You have all sorts of excuses for things don't you,
Laney?"

He won't face me so all that I can see is the side
of his face and the mound of his swollen purple eye.

"I didn't know you were so mad about that. I tried
to come over to your house. You wouldn't let me in!"

It's no use blinking, the tears are running, and if
I'm not careful, all of the emotion and fear from the
past couple of weeks will come pouring out and I'll
never stop crying. I press my hands against my eyes.
My stupid hands. I wouldn't be sitting here if I hadn't
had to grab Lyle's hands at the gym that day.

The other kids are shouting to each other on the
playground around us. Axel's voice is the clearest,

calling to someone to throw a ball.

When the tears finally stop, I wipe my cheeks and pull my hands away.

"I thought we were friends," I say to Lyle. He tilts his chin toward the sky, leaning the back of his head against the brick wall, and takes a deep breath in and out.

"I think you should stay away from me," he says slowly.

"I should? Or you want me to?"

"Listen. It's better if you do. It's not a good idea to hang out with me. They'll all hate you, too, if they see you with me." He faces me, his tone kinder but still firm.

It's not funny, but I laugh. Maybe I'm relieved at his reason.

"Do I look like I fit in here, Lyle?" Three girls in pink sweatshirts and blonde ponytails walk past us. Lyle and I both look from them to my black T-shirt, jeans, and the drawings on my shoes. "They don't like me anyway. You're my first real friend since kindergarten." I think of Tabitha and Carmen, though I'm not sure if Carmen counts anymore. "At least the first real friend that's my age."

Lyle leans his head back again. He doesn't tell me to go away again, but he doesn't ask me to stay either.

I take a deep breath. "The last time I was friends with someone my age, it ended really badly, so I'm kind of hoping that doesn't happen here."

"What happened then?" Lyle asks.

"I was friends with Axel in kindergarten. He was actually nice back then. Before he turned into his awful self."

Lyle snorts. "I definitely wasn't expecting you to say that you were friends with Axel."

"Yeah, well, he was really different then. And he's hated me since then anyway, so it's not like being friends with you is going to make it worse."

Sitting this close, I can see the varying colors of purple around Lyle's eye, edged in a yellowish green. Green ochre.

"He did that to you, didn't he?" I know the answer, but I need to hear it from Lyle.

The wiry muscles in his arm tense beside me.

"You need to tell someone about this. I will if you don't."

It's the wrong thing to say.

"Stay away from me, Laney. I mean it. It's none of your business," he says, loud enough to be heard over the bell signaling us to return to our classroom.

"Lyle—"

He stands up. "Sorry if you have bad luck with your friendships, but we're not friends anymore. Okay?"

I watch the back of his gray T-shirt as he walks into the building.

"Good luck without me, Lyle Bertrand," I say. I know he can't hear me and I don't mean it anyway. Who was I kidding to think that I could protect him? What is my big plan anyway, to stay with him and watch out for fires? To threaten Axel? From now on, I'll worry about protecting myself. And I'll stay as far away from Lyle as possible.

After school, I rush out the door. I want to leave before Lyle does. I don't want to worry about whether he's walking or biking and if Axel is following him.

Frida jumps out from behind the grass when I

start down the path. I scoop her up in my arms.

"Tabitha's right to prefer cats to people," I tell her. She purrs in response and then wiggles to get down.

Frida weaves in and out of the grass in front of me as I walk. It's too quiet, leaving my brain too much room to make its own noise with thoughts about Carmen and Walt and Lyle and Axel. I pick a piece of grass and try to remember Lyle's instructions. I blow on it, but it sounds like a tire leaking air.

I'm grateful when I finally arrive at Tabitha's. I half expect her to be laying on the lawn chair on her back porch covered in cats, but the porch is empty. Even though I know it's silly, I'm momentarily disappointed. I could use an afternoon with Tabitha, chatting while sipping lavender tea.

I lift the amethyst-colored flower pot to find the key. A crackling in the bushes next to the porch breaks the silence. The bush shakes violently.

I freeze, one hand holding the flower pot, the other holding the key. I hear the crackling noise again, louder this time.

"Who is that?" I ask. Frida tilts her head at me.

"Who is that?" I repeat. The bush continues to shake.

"Who's in there?" I cling tightly to the flowerpot.

The crackling stops and footsteps pound on the dirt behind the bush. It's the sounds of someone running away.

I stand up on one of Tabitha's porch chairs, peering over the bush. There's nothing but dust and dry grass. Was I imagining things? The bush quivers and a small black cat steps out from under it, shaking dust off her fur.

"Silly cat, you scared me," I say. I try to convince myself that I only heard rustling. Maybe I imagined the footsteps. My heart bangs against my chest. I step down from the chair and lean toward the bush. Caught in its branches is a half empty bag of Doritos.

Chapter Sixteen

———

THE NEXT MORNING, I CAN'T GET OUT OF
bed. It's as if the stress of Carmen leaving,
the hidden painting in the tree house, the
future flash of the fire, and the possibility that Axel
followed me to Tabitha's has melded into a hard knot
in my stomach. I try to sit up but feel as if a bowling
ball is pressing against me. I can't budge. Walt clamors around the kitchen, banging pots together to make
coffee and eggs. Usually that's all it takes to get me out
of bed.

"Laney!" Walt calls when I don't appear.

"Mmmph," I groan in response.

Walt opens my door, holding a steaming mug.
"You getting up today?" he asks.

"I can't," I tell him, staring at the ceiling. There's a

crack in the shape of a lopsided heart. I never noticed it before.

Walt sits on the bed next to me. He presses a warm hand to my forehead.

"Do you feel okay?"

"My stomach hurts."

"You think you need to stay home?"

I nod. Walt wrinkles his brow.

"So, here's the thing. I have a meeting with a potential client today for a huge house project. Normally I'd just take the day off and stay here with you, but I don't know if I can miss—"

"It's okay. I'll be fine here."

"Are you sure? I hate to leave you alone." He hesitates. "I could try calling Carmen."

"No, really, I'm okay. It's not so bad. I just need to rest a little."

Walt leans down and kisses my forehead.

"I'll call the school to let them know you're sick. And I'll call you later to check up on you, okay?"

When I hear the rumble of Walt's motor as he drives away, the weight lifts a little bit. I try sitting up again and find that I can. Something scratches at the windowsill. Frida is balancing on the ledge, her breath making white clouds on the glass. When I open the window, a blast of cold air follows her in. Frida jumps down onto my bed and curls up.

I'm feeling well enough to get dressed so I pull on my jeans and shirt. When I reach for my sweatshirt, I remember my favorite old sweatshirt, balled up in the back of the closet. I dig it out and inspect it. The blood is gone, but I still think of Lyle.

"Forget about him," I say out loud, pulling the sweatshirt over my head.

Sitting at the kitchen table, I take a sip of the luke-warm coffee Walt left in his mug and nearly spit it out. I eye the plate he left for me, but the thought of cold scrambled eggs turns my stomach. I give up on breakfast. Crossing my arms on the table and resting my head on them, I picture Walt reading the yellow paper that day when I came home from school.

Then it occurs to me. The yellow paper is some-where in the house.

I stand up and scour the kitchen. Cabinets filled with mismatched plates and cups; a junk drawer stuffed with dried out pens, spare change, and Walt's

Magee Construction business cards; a shelf piled with Play-Doh cans; and a fridge that's too empty since Carmen stopped coming for dinner. There's no place for Walt to hide anything in here. I walk through the living room, past the empty stove, past my Sleeping Beauty drawing, past the television and the sagging couch. Every object in our house is suddenly suspicious—a potential hiding place. My room and the bathroom are out. That leaves Walt's room.

His door creaks when I push it open. I whip around, but of course Frida is the only one to hear the noise. She yawns and stretches on my bed. A cloud must be passing over the sun because the house becomes dark and then bright again.

I look around Walt's room. The walls are covered in framed drawings and paintings that I've made for him over the years. The bowling ball weight expands in my belly for a moment. Walt has always been good to me, has always loved me. He has also always respected my privacy. I think about my tree house and how he has never once asked to come inside since he built it for me. I can't imagine him going through my things without asking me first.

Over his bed is a framed painting that's nearly as wide as I am tall. I made it when I was nine years old on the back porch while Carmen and Walt sat in chairs talking and watching me, responding to my questions about whether Carmen wanted to be wearing a red or blue dress (red) and whether Walt's eyes are closer to gray or blue (gray). In the painting, Walt stands to one side, his baseball hat on his head and his tool belt around his waist. I'm in the middle holding his hand. Carmen is holding my other hand and I'm looking up at her, a huge red smile on my face.

I remember that day and the way the wind kept blowing the paper I was painting until Walt put a rock on each corner to hold it down. Then suddenly I remember something else.

I remember Walt leaning back in his chair and saying to Carmen, "She's such a talented painter. She gets that from her mother."

I stopped painting when he said that, holding a paintbrush coated with yellow paint in my hand. You can see the drips coming down from the sun on the painting now, where I held the wet brush over the paper for too long.

"My mother?" I asked him, not turning around.

"Oh, I meant my mother," he said. "My mother was quite a painter." And yet Walt had never talked about his mother painting and I'd never seen anything she'd ever done. Of course, she had died when he was young and he never talked about her much, so maybe this was something new I didn't know. But later, when I asked if he had kept any of his mother's paintings, Walt looked confused.

"My mother? An artist? She was a great lady who could run a farm and chop wood like nobody's business, but I don't think she ever picked up a paintbrush, Laney, unless maybe it was to paint the side of a house."

I take a step into his room. Then another. Soon I am pulling open the drawers of his dresser, pushing aside white undershirts and heavy flannels. Like me, he doesn't care much for variety in clothing, so it doesn't take long to find that there's nothing else in there. The trunk at the end of his bed contains two wool blankets and some sweaters. I shake out the blankets and run my hand along the wood at the bottom, getting nothing but a splinter in my palm for my efforts.

With my heart pounding, I sit down on his bed and look at the bedside table. A phone and a lamp sit on top of the table. I've never opened the drawer. If it's not in there, my search is over. I can't imagine anywhere else it could be.

I pick at the splinter in my palm, not sure which I'm dreading more—finding the letter or not finding the letter. After a hard tug, the splinter comes out.

The knob on the drawer stares up at me like an accusing eye. What am I waiting for?

I wipe my sweaty hands off on my jeans and reach to grab the knob. This is it. I pull on the drawer. It sticks. I have to wriggle it, holding onto the lamp with one hand so it won't crash to the floor. I give the drawer one more tug and it comes flying out, hurling me backwards. The contents of the drawer scatter across the room and land with a clatter on the floor. Keys, ChapStick, two pens, and a faded yellow envelope.

Chapter Seventeen

———

I DON'T BOTHER WITH THE DRAWER OR THE other contents. I grab the envelope with trembling hands. The paper inside is torn slightly along the creases and nearly rips when I unfold it. There are grease marks on the sides of the page. The ink is smeared, but still legible.

I read:

Dear Walt,

This is Elaine. She is our daughter.

I stop reading there. *Our* daughter. Walt *is* my father. For all these years, I never believed him. But why would I believe him? He told me that he and my mom were happily married and that my mom died when I was a baby. Why would my mom be writing him a note and leaving me out in the cold? I continue:

I'm sorry. For everything. For leaving you at the wedding, for disappearing like that, for not calling, for not telling you about her . . . I don't expect you to forgive me, but I hope you will believe me. I don't want things to be this way.

I love her and you very, very much.

I read that line again. *Then why did you leave me?* I want to scream, but there's no one to hear.

It's about the fire, Walt. When I touched your hands at our wedding, I had that same vision. I thought it would go away when I left, I thought maybe I could save her by taking her away from you, but nothing changed. As soon as she was born and I touched her, I saw the fire again. I can't raise her knowing how it ends.

I am leaving her for you. Please don't try to contact me. Tell Elaine that she had a mother who loved her very much. Tell her that I died when she was just a baby.

I hope you two will be happy together. I know you'll be a good father. Keep her away from fire. Maybe without me she'll be safe.

It's better this way.

I love you.

Aster

Across the bottom, the stationery is printed with the words:

Aster Lazos, Artist, 917-555-0281

They lied. Together, my parents lied to me. I've spent my whole life believing that some stranger left me and that Walt took me in and wasn't even my dad. I want to tear the letter to pieces. Instead, I ball it up and throw it at the wall. It hits with an unsatisfying whisper.

Walt is my father and Aster Lazos is my mother. The words repeat in my head over and over until they stop making sense and simply become words, jumbled and disconnected.

Aster Lazos. There's more than just her name written at the bottom of the letter.

I grab the balled up letter and smooth it out on the bed. There's a tear now along one of the creases.

Aster Lazos, Artist, 917-555-0281

I pick up the phone. *Don't think*, I tell myself, *just dial*. With shaking hands, I dial the number and wait for my mother's phone to ring.

"The number you have dialed has been disconnected," an automatic voice announces on the other line.

I am shaking so hard that it takes me two tries to put the phone back on the receiver. I'm shaking as hard as Lyle did on the porch the other day, only I'm not cold.

I look at her name again. Lazos. Walt had never mentioned her last name before. Why does that sound familiar?

Suddenly I can picture it perfectly. The small crimped writing at the bottom of the painting of the baby. Lazos.

I stuff the paper in my pocket. Leaving the envelope and mess on Walt's floor, I rush outside.

The rungs to the tree house are covered in a thin layer of frost. When I get to the top, I rub my hands together to warm them and then flip the painting around. Before, I hardly noticed the signature. Now that one word means everything. Lazos. Aster Lazos painted this. This is my mother's painting.

I stick the canvas under my arm and climb back down the tree house. Once again I find myself running across the fields to Lyle's house. This time I don't care about the stinging in my legs or the burning in my lungs as I suck in the cool air. *Walt is my father and Aster Lazos is my mother.*

Lyle's mom's rusty white Toyota is parked in the driveway when I approach the house. She's home. Once again, I race up the front steps and pound on the door. This time I'm not giving up. This time I *know* it's a painting of me and Lyle's not here to stop me from asking about it. I bang against the door, but no one answers. That's okay, I was expecting that. I bang and bang until my fist aches, and then I pound some more. The door rattles under my fist and the sound of my knocking echoes across the hills.

"Let me in! Please let me in!" I shout.

If she's listening, Lyle's mom doesn't respond. The blinds don't move.

"Let me in!" I continue to cry, still beating against the door. The knot from this morning starts to grow again in my stomach. It hardens and presses against my insides until I have to sit down. I slump against the back of the door, still clutching the painting. She's not going to answer.

The sun reflects against the window above me and I consider trying to push the window open to crawl through, but the thought of moving at all exhausts me. I place the painting on the stoop and curl up in a ball. I close my eyes, willing the pain in my stomach to go away. Instead, it spreads through my whole body. I curl up tighter against the cold air and wait for the sun to warm me, but it lacks its usual heat today. The bristly fingers of the welcome mat scratch my cheek, but I don't move. As cold and uncomfortable as I am, I drift off into a deep, dreamless sleep.

Chapter Eighteen

———

"ASTER! OH, ASTER!" A VOICE I DON'T recognize cuts through my sleep. Someone is shaking me awake. I struggle to open one eye and see a hand on my shoulder. When I close my eye again, I'm not dreaming. I'm having a future flash.

I'm sitting in a sunny living room with a canvas and easel in front of me, a paintbrush in one hand. The canvas in front of me is wet with paint. I study the three glistening apples, one of them on its side. Did I really paint that? It's better than anything I've painted before.

"Nice work, Laney," someone says. I peer around my canvas and see two floral couches and a coffee table. The coffee table is covered with a white sheet and has three apples perched atop it. Then I notice another canvas across from mine. Paint-splattered jeans stick out beneath it. A face peaks out from behind the canvas. A pale, moon-shaped face.

Lyle's mom.

My eyes fly open. The same pale face from my future flash is peering down at me, filling my vision. She looks like a washed out version of Lyle. Faint freckles mark her ghostly skin and her hair hangs to her shoulders, a drab, greasy version of Lyle's red. She's wearing a stained beige bathrobe.

"You look just like her," she whispers, her eyes widening. "Exactly like her, but with gray eyes instead of brown . . ."

"Exactly like . . .?"

"Aster, you look like Aster. It's uncanny really, the—"

"So, you know my mom?"

"Oh child, I'm so sorry I didn't let you in earlier. I am not myself these days. Can you get up? Let me help you get up and you can come in from the cold so we can talk."

She steps back so that I can stand, raising her eyebrows when I grab the painting. I look at the canvas and then back at her.

"I took this," I say, stating the obvious. "I'm sorry."

"No, no, it's okay. I'm sorry. Come in, come in."

I follow her into the house. It takes my eyes a moment to adjust, as the blinds are pulled shut against the light. Inside, it smells like mildewed towels and stale toast. Then I realize we're in a darkened version of the living room from my future flash—the same floral couches and coffee table, minus the sunlight and apples.

"Sit down," she says, patting the couch. "Let me get you something. Water? Soda? I'm afraid we don't have much."

"Water's fine," I tell her, as she pads barefoot into the kitchen. I'm tempted to open the blinds and crack the windows when she's in the other room, as the air in the house feels heavy and the lack of sunlight is making me feel claustrophobic. Instead, I finger the paper in my pocket and wait.

Lyle's mom returns and hands me a chipped glass with SoHo 36 Gallery printed in bright yellow on the side. How did a woman with a shed full of incredible art and a glass from a New York City gallery end up in Thornville?

"I'm Helen," she says, sitting down. "And you must be Elaine."

"People call me Laney."

Helen smacks her forehead with her palm. "I can't believe I didn't put two and two together. Lyle has been talking about a girl named Laney, but I didn't think . . . Laney, Elaine . . . of course! Here you were knocking at my door!"

This makes no sense to me but she doesn't explain further. She simply shakes her head. I have so many questions to ask her but I don't know where to begin. I take a sip of water to give myself something to do. The house is as void of sound as it is of light.

Helen clears her throat, looks at me, and then averts her eyes. "I'm sorry again that I didn't let you in. I know you're Lyle's only friend here and I thought you might think badly of him, what with me . . . well." She waves her hand vaguely over her stained robe. "But I had no idea you were Aster's daughter!"

I had no idea either, I think.

"I found this painting in your shed," I say, touching the edge of the canvas. "I've been wanting to ask you about it. I know it's me."

Helen tucks a strand of hair behind her ear. We both look at the painting. Then the words begin to tumble out of her again.

"It's you, yes, your mother painted that. She gave that to me years ago. It made her too sad. She was an amazing artist. And she loved you very much, you know. She never stopped loving you."

"I didn't know anything about my mother until today."

"Nothing?"

"I never asked. Walt, I mean, um, my dad told me she died when I was a baby."

Helen coughs into her hand, perhaps trying to hide her surprise. She stares at the blank wall across the room. With all those incredible paintings in the shed, all of the walls in the house are empty. I wait for her to continue and, when she doesn't say anything, I begin to worry that she's forgotten I'm here at all. Then, to my relief, she continues.

"I'm sorry, I'm lost in memories is all. And I'll confess I haven't talked to anyone besides Lyle for a while. It's been a tough couple of years. Anyway, I

should start at the beginning. Your mother. Hank and
I—"

"Hank?"

"Sorry, that's Lyle's father. We had just moved to
New York City. He was in school there and I was painting. But we had a new baby and we had no money,
just barely scraping by. So we decided to find someone else to share our apartment with us. A friend told
me about another artist who had recently moved to
the city and was looking for a place to live. We hit it
off immediately. She was funny and kind and incred-
ibly talented, though she had a sadness to her."

"What does she look like?"

"She looked almost exactly like you," Helen says,
shaking her head as if she can't get over the resem-
blance. "Oh! Hold on a second." She gets up. She is
gone for so long I begin to think she's not coming
back.

"Here," she says, when she finally returns to the
room. She hands me a picture in a silver frame. I
study the picture of two women standing next to a
colorful abstract painting. One woman has pale skin
and red hair and is smiling at the camera; the other

has thick black hair and is pointing at the painting, her face partially hidden by her hair.

"Hank took this of me and Aster at one of my openings years ago," Helen says. I look more closely at the woman with black hair. My mother. Though I can't see her face clearly, there's something about the line of her chin and shape of her longish nose that reminds me of the face I see every time I look in the mirror.

I don't want to ask, but I know I have to. "What do you mean she *looked* like me?"

"Oh," Helen says, tucking a stray strand of hair behind her ear again. "I'm sorry, Elaine, Laney. Your mother passed away three years ago."

I look back at the picture in front of me and try to take it all in. This morning, I had no idea who my mother was. Now I had discovered her and lost her in a matter of hours.

"Why? How?"

"She was in a car accident. She moved out of New York City nine years ago to a small town in upstate New York, near Lake Champlain. She wanted to get away from people, from the world. She was driving on an icy road one night and she crashed into a tree."

The stale air in the room feels like it's choking me. I know it's rude, but I can't help it. I turn around and pull the chord on the blinds. Dust particles dance as the sunlight streams across the room. I push up against the window and open it a crack, feeling better as soon as the cool, fresh air pours through. If Helen disapproves, she doesn't say anything.

"Why did she want to get away from everyone?" I ask, sinking back into the couch.

"She had trouble being too close with people. I guess after losing her and my husband in the same year, I can relate a little bit. Sometimes it's easier to hold people at a distance. I guess that's why Lyle and I have been moving around so much. I keep hoping things will be better, but of course they're the same everywhere we go. Your mother and my husband died within weeks of each other. It shattered my world."

I take in Helen's stained bathrobe and greasy hair and think about Lyle coming home every day to this stuffy house. I think of Walt lying to me.

"It's not fair, just doing what's easier," I tell her. "It's not fair to the people around you, the people who should be close to you, people who need you."

"It's not," Helen agrees. "I haven't been a good mother to Lyle these past few years. I keep uprooting him and taking him from one place to another. You know, he was the one who suggested Colorado. He met your mother years ago and remembered that she spoke fondly of it here. He didn't know about you. I had no idea whether you were still here, but I asked him, the first day of school, if there was a girl named Elaine in his class, but he said no. I never made the connection with Laney . . ." She shakes her head. "No, I haven't been a good mother lately."

"My mom left me on a stoop in the cold," I remind her.

"It's true," Helen says. "And I can't even imagine how that must feel. But try to understand. You see, Aster had a special reason for struggling with people." She pauses and bites her lip, as if trying to decide something.

"What do you mean?"

"I know this might sound crazy to you, but she believed that she had . . . visions. She claimed she saw things about people, about the future. She found out she was pregnant with you on the day she married your father. When she touched his hand at the wedding, she saw a vision of him next to a huge fire. Wanting to protect you, she left him before even telling him she was pregnant. When you were born, she saw you in the fire too. Only you didn't make it out. Most people would probably ignore those visions, but for some reason she really believed they were going to come true. She couldn't take loving you and believing that she was going to lose you in a fire. It broke her heart to do it, but she left you with your father to escape those terrible visions. That's when she moved to New York."

I remember the note in my pocket. *It's about the fire, Walt. When I touched your hands at our wedding, I had that same vision. I thought it would go away when I left, I thought maybe I could save her by taking her away from you, but nothing changed. As soon as she was born and I touched her, I saw the fire again.* I had been so overwhelmed with discovering the identity of my parents and being angry at their deceit that I somehow didn't fully register this important information. My mother had future flashes, just like me. And just like me, she saw a fire.

"What time is it?" I ask, wiping my suddenly sweaty palms on my jeans.

"Time?" She's clearly thrown off. She stumbles as she stands up to check the clock in the kitchen. "Four fifteen. Lyle should actually be home by now," she says, sitting back on the couch and picking nervously at a hangnail. "He keeps having these bike accidents. I know it's silly, but I get a little worried when he's running late."

"What was he wearing today?" I ask.

"Wearing? You want to know what he was wearing?" Her forehead wrinkles.

"Please."

"Oh, I don't know. Let's see. Some jeans? His gray T-shirt? That shirt was the last gift his father gave him and he wears it pretty much every—"

"I have to go." I stand so abruptly that I knock the water glass over next to me. It spills on the table and sloshes onto the floor.

Helen jumps in her seat, startled by my sudden movement. "I'm not sure I under—"

"You'll let me in next time I come back?" I ask,

hating to leave with so many questions unanswered.

"Oh, of course. I should have, I mean, I would have before. It's just that I haven't been up to—"

I don't wait to hear her explanation. I leave the painting of me on the couch and bolt out the door.

It's not until I'm almost a mile from Lyle's house that it occurs to me that in my unnerved state, I wasn't thinking clearly. I should have asked Helen to give me a ride. Helen mentioned Lyle's bike accidents, so I know that he biked to school today, which means he should be returning on the road. Remembering the letter and my mother's vision of the fire had caused me to panic, imagining that he wasn't showing up because he was caught in a fire. But he's not going to burst into flames in the middle of the road on the way home from school. The real danger is that he's late because of Axel. And what am I going to do if I see Axel attacking him? Nothing. There's nothing I'd be able to do. Should I turn around and get Helen to come with me? But what if he's just running late for no reason? Lyle told me to stay away from him. How would he feel about me racing down the road with his mom looking for him? These thoughts churn as I run.

I'm thinking as I pound down the long stretch of flat road and I'm thinking when I pass the dusty spot where Axel knocked Lyle off his bike and I'm still thinking about those questions when I reach the top of the hill and look down and see the school. No-where between the school and me is a boy on a bike.

I stop running and walk the rest of the way to school. There's no rush now. Lyle must not have biked after all. Maybe his mom didn't notice that he left his bike at home today. He probably took the path home. He's probably pushing open his front door right now. I tell myself this, but don't quite believe it.

When I arrive at the school and see his bike still chained to the bike rack, I know it's not true.

Chapter Nineteen

——————

THE SCHOOL BUILDING IS EMPTY. I TRY opening the back door, but it's locked. When I run around to the front door, I notice another bike leaning against the side of the building. Axel's bike. Maybe Axel started beating up on Lyle in the schoolyard and someone intervened? Again, I don't quite believe my own thoughts, but allow myself a kernel of hope as I race up the front steps of the school and pull on the front door handle. It doesn't budge. For the second time today, I find myself banging on a door.

After a while, I give up and sit on the stoop. My legs are tired from running and I need to think. There's no use running off when I have no idea which direction to go.

Where could they be? I tug at the tear in my jeans. An empty plastic bag blows around the parking lot. It looks like a dancing ghost, moving up and down and back and forth in the air. I can hear Ms. Fontane's voice in my head saying, "Three steps, left, right, left." What did I see in the gym that day? I press my palms against my eyes. There was so much smoke blocking any vision of my surroundings. But there had to be some sort of clue. We were inside somewhere. And I tripped over something, something soft that bumped against my shins.

"A cat!" I yell, jumping up.

I dash across the parking lot to the back of the school and then down the cracked dirt path. I'm nearly to the hill when I hear a familiar sound. A shrill noise, like a loud whistle—like Lyle blowing against a piece of grass. I stop and listen again. It's coming from the direction of Tabitha's house.

I pluck a piece of grass and put my fingers around it like Lyle taught me. I bring it to my lips and then hesitate. Helen's voice repeats in my head: "She saw you in the fire, too. Only you didn't make it out." What am I running toward? Do I really want to find

Lyle? If my future flashes always come true, does that mean my mom's future flash will also? The shrill noise pierces the air again. My mom left me to deal with this on my own. I can't do the same to Lyle. I take a deep breath and blow. To my surprise, a piercing sound fills the air. A second later, another whistle responds. I am running again.

When I get close to Tabitha's house, I scan the roof for smoke and fire. My legs nearly crumple in relief when I see none. Then I see Lyle. Or at least I guess it's Lyle because of his gray T-shirt and red hair, but his face looks entirely different. His eye is still swollen and purple from the other day, but now the other eye is swollen too and his nose is a blood-smeared bulge. He's pacing back and forth across the porch, his hands on his head, taking deep breaths.

"What happened to you?" I cry.

"Axel," he says.

When I step onto the porch, he stops pacing and starts talking so quickly that I can barely keep up. "When you were home sick today, I thought I'd come feed the cats. I found the key next to the pot, which seemed kinda weird, but then I thought maybe you forgot to put the pot back over it the last time you came. I let myself in and I didn't know it, but he was already inside. I think he was burning those GI Joes on Tabitha's bed because there was a weird chemical smell coming from the bedroom." Lyle's voice sounds strange, like he's holding his nose, his n's sounding like d's. As he talks, he keeps eyeing the glass door behind him. "Anyway, I didn't know what it was but I went into the kitchen and then I heard a noise upstairs. I grabbed a cat bowl—it was the closest hard object I could find—and I climbed the stairs. I thought it was probably just a cat knocking something over but I wanted to be sure. I got to the landing and Axel was walking out of Tabitha's bedroom. He saw me and he did this." Lyle points to his nose.

"Did you talk to him at all? I mean, before he—"

"I asked him what he was doing in Tabitha's house. He told me it was none of my business and then I said he had to get out. That's when he punched me."

"I can't believe he broke into Tabitha's house and then broke your nose!" I don't know why anything Axel does shocks me anymore, but somehow this does.

"I don't know if my nose is necessarily brok—"

"It's broken," I interrupt. "There's no question. It barely even looks like a nose."

Lyle winces. "I knew this would happen. If not today, then tomorrow. Axel came up to me at school, you know. He asked me why my, uh, girlfriend wasn't there."

My face flushes.

"Then he said he doesn't like people spying on him, and I told him that he already gave me a black eye to prove that point. Then I said that he's crazy to think that I was spying on him since he would never do anything interesting enough to be worth spying on."

"You said that to him? How did you get away with him not punching you right then?"

"Good question. He probably wanted to. A whole bunch of kids were listening. But Ms. Fontane interrupted. She got us right back to doing pliés." Lyle starts pacing again. "Still, I just don't get how he knew about Tabitha's house. I mean, he got here before I did so he couldn't have followed me."

I close my eyes and picture the Dorito bag caught in the bush's branches. The bush that I can almost touch from where we are.

"Axel followed me here yesterday," I say. "He must have figured out that no one is home and thought no one would be here because I wasn't at school." I look at Lyle's nose and wonder what would have happened if I had come instead of Lyle. Axel might hate me, but he's never physically hurt me. Did he punch Lyle because Lyle caught him in Tabitha's house? Or because Lyle stood up to him today? Or just to do it, like all the other times? Then I realize all that matters is that it has to stop.

"Lyle, you have to tell someone." I take a deep breath. "Or I will. I mean it. I don't care if you hate me and don't want to be friends. He's going to kill you if we don't stop him."

"Yeah, I'm sorry I said that before about the whole friend thing. You're right. I should have told someone a long time ago. And I will. I promise. It's just, well, there's another more immediate problem with Axel."

"Where is he?" I ask, as Lyle glances at the door again.

"That's the thing," Lyle says and then hesitates. "He's in the house."

"What? We need to get out of here before he—"

"I don't think he's going to come out. I fell down when he punched me, but when I stood up, I hit him over the head with that." He points down and I notice the sparkly purple ceramic cat bowl on the porch.

"What?"

"He's knocked out in there. Upstairs, in the hall," Lyle says, pointing to the door. I look from Lyle to the cat bowl to the door, trying to take it all in.

"You knocked out Axel Johnson with a cat bowl?" is all I can think to say.

"He's not moving, but he's breathing," Lyle replies, looking back at the house.

"We need to get help right away. It's at least half a mile to the closest house and we can't drag him that far. Not to mention that he'd probably kill us if he woke up while we were dragging him. Wait a sec. I'll call Walt. I'll explain what happened . . ."

"You're going to call Walt?"

"You have a better idea?" I ask.

"No, I guess you're right."

"Hopefully he won't wake up while we're looking for the phone."

"I'm going to try not to think about that," Lyle says.

When we step into the house, the putrid odor of cat urine is overwhelming. Despite the cat door, apparently Frida is the only cat going outside with Tabitha out of town. I look around the living room and see dozens of cats, but no phone. No phone in the kitchen either. Suddenly I remember Tabitha talking to her friend on her plum-colored cell phone.

"There's no phone in the house," I whisper.

"Okay, let's get out of here then. Your comment about Axel waking up doesn't exactly make me want to stick around."

"Hold on. Do you smell that?"

"Do you really think I can smell anything with my nose like this?" Lyle asks. "But I'm guessing it smells like cat pee. Surprise, surprise."

"No, there's something else."

"Maybe that chemical smell I noticed before?" Lyle asks.

I wrinkle my nose and step past Lyle toward the stairs. The cat odor no longer masks the strange smell.

"Smoke," I say, sniffing again. I try to keep the rising panic out of my voice. "I think it's smoke."

"Don't go up there, Laney. That's where Axel is," Lyle says.

"I don't want to, but that smell—"

There's nothing good upstairs, but I trudge up the steps anyway.

At the top of the staircase, I take a deep breath and poke my head into the hall. I look to my right and see nothing but a door at the end of the hallway. Tabitha's sewing room. I look the other way.

Axel is laying on his stomach with his face turned to the side. My heart beats so loud I'm sure I'll wake him. I take a few steps down the hall. His white-blonde hair is flopped over his face, sticking to some blood on his cheek. His shirt moves up and down. He's breathing, but otherwise doesn't budge. I feel a moment of pity for the boy laying on the floor. Then I hear a noise behind me. Lyle's battered face appears in the door frame at the top of the stairs.

I raise my eyebrows at Lyle.

"That's him," he whispers.

"No kidding."

I didn't come up here to risk rousing Axel. I came up because of the smell, much stronger now, coming from the room behind him. I walk past Axel, careful not to bump into him.

The door to Tabitha's room is open.

Please don't be what I think this is.

I close my eyes for a minute before peering in. Instead of the usual purple patchwork quilt, furious yellow flames and thick swirling smoke cover her bed. The fire leaps to Tabitha's purple curtains. It devours them in an instant. A wave of heat slams against my face. I take a step back and bump against the wall.

"Run!" Lyle yells, turning back toward the stairs.

"Wait! We can't leave him here!" I lean down and tug on one of Axel's black high top sneakers. It comes off in my hand. I grab onto Axel's leg, but he's too heavy to move by myself.

Smoke pours into the hallway now, above our heads. A flame jumps from the room and lands on the rug. It races down the carpet quicker than I would have thought possible.

"Laney! C'mon!" Lyle yells.

I take a step toward Lyle and trip over a cat. I

sprawl forward. Fire sears my hand. The pain is far more intense than it was in my future flash. Blisters instantly erupt on the reddened skin of my palm, and I pull myself up, screaming.

It is happening. The future flash I saw when I first touched Lyle is no longer a future flash. The nightmare of fire and blood is my real life.

I glance down the hall. I am terrified. I can run for the stairs, like I did in my future flash, or I can find the courage to stay and try to save the life of someone who used to be my friend. I know what I have to do. I didn't choose to come here so I could just run away. I'm not going to be like my mother. Maybe it's hopeless, maybe I won't be able to change what happens to us, but I have to at least try.

I pull my shirt over my mouth and use my free hand to grab Axel's arm. He doesn't budge. Lyle pauses at the top of the stairs, looking back at me.

"I can't move him by myself!" I yell.

Lyle rushes to me. Together, we flip Axel over. His eyes flutter open and then close again.

"Under his arm!" I yell. Lyle is bent over, coughing up blood. I panic and reconsider running. There's no point in trying to help Axel if it means all three of us might die.

Lyle reaches under Axel's arm. I let my shirt fall from my mouth and hold onto Axel with both hands, pain blasting through my blisters.

We can't do this, I think with each step, but somehow we keep pulling. Smoke fills my lungs until I can barely breathe. The rug behind us is now on fire. Axel's leg is burning too.

"Stop!" I scream to Lyle. A fist-sized flame is eating through Axel's jeans. I drop Axel's foot and stomp out the flame.

"We need to get out of here," Lyle wheezes. I grab Axel's leg again. When I glance down at him, I notice that he's staring back at me, his pale blue eyes wide with fear and confusion.

"Lyle!" I scream.

Lyle looks down and drops Axel's leg. For a second, no one moves.

Then Axel pushes himself up, his body erecting slowly like some huge bloody creature rising from the deep. He steadies himself against the wall. Then he lurches forward. I flinch, but Axel doesn't even look at me or Lyle. He heads for the staircase, the only way out.

Then it comes to me—the one future flash I had of Axel. It replays in my head in an instant. It happened in kindergarten on the day we were trying to recreate strawberry astronaut ice cream in Carmen's bakery. We both had wanted to stir the sticky pink mixture so Carmen suggested that we stir it together. We grabbed onto the wooden spoon at the same time. When his hand touched mine, I saw the hallway. This hallway. These stairs. An older boy and a white cat with black ears. I followed the boy down the stairs.

Then, in the future flash, came a crash.

And darkness.

A cool sensation washed over me, like a late afternoon breeze in the fall. The kind that tells you that snow is blowing in.

The darkness I experienced in that future flash was almost peaceful, which is probably why I didn't remember it until now.

Axel takes another step toward the stairs and it hits me. I know what's going to happen.

"We'll die," I whisper it first. Then louder. "My mother saw it and I saw it too. We will die! Axel, we all will die if we go down the stairs! We need to find another way out!"

He turns to me, bleary-eyed. He clearly doesn't understand.

"Laney, it's the only way out," Lyle says from behind me.

"No, Axel, stop!" I scream, tears choking me. "Don't go that way! Please, that's the wrong way!"

"Laney, what are you talking about," Lyle says. Axel is leaning against the wall, barely able to stand. The heat is unbearable and the smoke thick around our heads.

"Lyle, Axel, listen. You have to trust me. If we go that way, we're going to die."

"Look, Art Freak," Axel says before more billows of thick, black smoke send him into a coughing fit.

I grab his arm. His muscles scare me, but I hold on tight.

"I saw this," I say, gripping tighter. "You have to believe me. I don't have time to explain, but I saw this and if we go down those stairs we're going to die."

"Laney, that's crazy," Lyle manages through a cough. "We've got to get out of here."

"Fine!" I cry. "There's going to be a white cat with black ears in front of that stairway in a second. I swear."

We all look at the stairway entrance.

"There's no cat," Axel says as he makes another move toward the stairs. I reach out and grab Axel's shirt, but he pulls away.

"Laney!" Lyle yells. "We have to get out of here. Now!"

"It's true, I swear it!" I yell, but they're not listening. I can barely breathe through the smoke and tears. I don't have a choice. I have to tell them the truth.

"The picture," I say. "The one I drew of you in the fire! I saw it, Lyle. I knew this would happen!"

That's when the cat appears.

"There," I say, pointing frantically at the black-and-white cat.

"Where do we go then?" Lyle asks.

"This way," I say. "There's a way out this way." To my relief, both Lyle and Axel follow me. I have no idea where I'm going, really. All that I know is we're going away from the stairs.

I pull open the door to the room at the end of the hall—Tabitha's sewing room. It's decorated in purple, of course and filled with cloth, colored thread, and embroidered cat pillows.

"There," I point to the window at the far end of the room. "That's how we get out." We rush to the window and look down. There's a row of bushes underneath but not the kind that would cushion your fall. They are the kind with thorns and thick branches that could impale you.

Axel opens his mouth to say something. A crash interrupts him. We can't see it, but I know. Part of the floor in Tabitha's bedroom caved in. The floor would have landed on our heads if we had taken the stairs down to the living room below.

Lyle pushes past me and yanks at the window, wheezing and coughing as he strains to open it. It doesn't budge. Axel joins him and together they struggle with the stuck pane.

"C'mon, c'mon," Axel says. The window gives suddenly with a shriek. Axel punches the screen out and it lands on the bushes below. We all stick our heads out to feel the cool, clean air against our faces.

"Go," Axel says, looking at me.

"Yeah, go, Laney," Lyle coughs.

"No. I'm going last. You guys go." I came here to save Lyle from the fire. I'm not going to have gone through all this for him to still burn up in this house.

No one moves.

"Go!" I scream.

Another crash echoes through the hall. Lyle and I back up and Axel swings his legs up over the window-sill and jumps. He lands hard just beyond the bushes and stumbles forward before falling, face down, into the grass.

"Go," I repeat to Lyle. Lyle pulls himself up and then hesitates on the windowsill for a second before he jumps. He lands with a scream. His foot twists un-naturally under him.

"Jump, Laney!" he yells to me, clutching his foot with his hands.

I pull myself up so that I'm sitting in the window-sill with my legs dangling below. The air is clear out-side. In front of me, the fields surrounding Tabitha's house appear to go on forever—the fields we'll need to walk through to get help.

Below me, Lyle and Axel don't look like they're walking any time soon, but at least they are alive.

I push myself off the windowsill and land smack in the middle of the bushes.

There are different types of pain. There's the kind that comes from watching your dad with his head down at the dinner table, too sad to eat, and there's the kind that comes from watching your best friend get thrown from his bike. Then there's the kind of pain that comes from dozens of sharp branches jabbing through your skin.

It's Lyle who hauls me from the bushes. Limping and wheezing, he drags me through the grass, the thorns still digging into my skin.

He lays me down, away from the house and near Axel. Then he collapses. Next to me, Axel groans but doesn't move.

I stare up at the sky. My vision is blurry and the pain from the thorns and from my burned hand doesn't let up, but for some reason I feel an overwhelming sense of relief. Then I remember.

We were supposed to die in the fire and we didn't. We changed that.

I changed that.

"We got out," I laugh and sob at the same time. "We escaped from the fire!"

"You saw it," Lyle says.

My head feels heavy and, for a second, I don't know what he's talking about.

"You saw it," Lyle repeats. "You saw the fire."

My relief disappears.

"I should have told someone. I should have told you," I try to say. I'm not sure if I say it loud enough. Lyle doesn't respond.

The blue sky above me fills with smoke. Thick, black smoke. I let this happen, I think. I got us out of the fire, but I let it get this far.

"I tried," I whisper.

The rasping noise next to me stops.

"Lyle?" I ask. I want to face him, but my body hurts too much.

Then the sweetest possible sound I could imagine cuts through the washed out noises around me—the sound of sirens. They are far away, but coming closer.

"We're going to be okay," I say to Lyle. He makes a gagging noise next to me. Then the world goes black.

Chapter Twenty

WHEN I OPEN MY EYES, I SEE A TUBE full of clear liquid attached to my left arm with a big Band-Aid. Instead of my black T-shirt, I'm wearing a baggy white hospital gown covered in spots the shape and color of lima beans. My arms are a map of bruises, scabs, and scratches. I breathe in. My lungs ache but the clean air fills them like it should. I'm in a bed next to a window. Walt is slumped in an uncomfortable looking chair at the end of my bed. When I attempt to sit up, his eyes fly open.

"Laney! Honey, you're awake." Ashes shake from his hair when he moves and his face is streaked with soot.

"You look terrible," I tell him. My throat feels scratchy and my voice sounds hoarse.

"Yeah, well, you don't look so hot yourself, kid," he says, but he's smiling.

I lift my hand to push the hair out of my eyes and notice that it is wrapped in gauze. The fire.

"Lyle!" I cry, kicking my legs to the side of the bed.

"Laney," Walt says, standing up, "Don't get up. You don't need to get up. Lyle's fine."

"He's okay?"

"He's just down the hall. He's being treated for smoke inhalation and some minor burns, just like you. He's also got a sprained ankle and a broken nose, but he'll be fine."

"Is Axel . . . ?"

"He's got burns on his leg and a pretty bad headache, but he's going to be okay."

I lay back and look out the window. I have a lot to ask Walt. But first I need to let him know what happened.

"Lyle didn't get the broken nose from the fire. Axel did that to him. He's been doing terrible things to him ever since Lyle moved here."

I move over a bit so Walt can sit on the side of my narrow bed.

"I know," Walt sighs. "Lyle explained the whole thing when he woke up. The police are talking to Axel's dad now."

"I should have told someone," I say, my eyes filling with tears.

Walt rubs his forehead with his hand. "You all are safe now and that's what's important. It could have been worse. It could have been much, much worse."

I close my eyes. What if Lyle had just told someone about what Axel was doing to him? What if *I* had just told someone? I kept thinking that I needed to protect Lyle when all I needed to do was tell someone the truth a long time ago. I think back to the day that Axel shoved Lyle off his bike and when Walt asked me about my drawing. If I had told Walt the truth then, the bullying would have stopped and the fire might never have happened. I am silent for a while, and then I whisper, "And Tabitha's house?"

"Her house is . . . gone Laney."

Part of me wants to cover my ears with my hands and bury myself under the covers, but questions keep bubbling up inside and I need to know the answers.

"What about Tabitha? Where will she live?"

"I talked to Tabitha on the phone and she won't be coming back to Thornville. She's going to stay with the friend she was visiting this week. Luckily her friend loves cats, too."

"So the cats—"

"Most of them made it out with you guys. The shelter is holding them for her and she'll be back to get them and take them away."

I pick at the gauze on my hand.

"What about Frida?" I whisper, almost afraid to ask.

"I've got good news. Frida was on your bed when I got home yesterday. She missed the whole thing."

As soon as he says it, I remember Frida balancing on the windowsill, her breath warm against the cool glass. Was that really just yesterday morning?

"I guess she'll be going to the shelter, too."

"Tabitha asked if you'd like to keep her and I told her I'm sure you would," Walt says.

"Really? I can keep her?"

"Of course, Laney. It's not a puppy, but I know you love that cat."

"She's better than a puppy!" I think about Frida,

warm and purring, sleeping on my bed every night. Then I imagine walking to school and passing a pile of gray ashes in place of Tabitha's purple home.

"I should have told someone," I repeat, on the verge of tears again. Walt and the room around me begin to swirl.

"Shh, Laney. It's okay. Don't worry about that. You need to rest."

A nurse comes in and before she reaches the bed, everything fades.

I wake up to a knock on the door. Walt is no longer sitting in the chair.

A nurse I don't recognize pokes her head in the room.

"Axel would like to speak to you. I will be here the whole time. Is it alright if he comes in for a second?"

I close my eyes, hoping I'm only dreaming. When I open them, the nurse is still there, waiting.

"Fine," I reply. "For a second."

Axel limps in and sits on Walt's chair. White gauze is wrapped around his head.

"Laney," he says and my whole body stiffens.

"Where's Walt?" I ask the nurse. "He should be here."

"He went to get something at the cafeteria. He'll be back in a minute. He hasn't left your side except to eat." I'm not sure what that means. How long have I been in the hospital? I can't help but wonder if Axel's dad has stayed with him this whole time, too.

The nurse stands in the doorway, talking softly with another aide.

"Why are you here?" I snap at Axel. He is the last person I want to see right now.

"I'm leaving so I just wanted to say, you know, bye."

"Oh."

"I'm leaving the hospital."

"That's good."

"And I won't be at school for a while."

"How come?" When I try to sit up the room tilts, so I lean back against my pillow.

"I'm going to live with my aunt for the rest of the school year. Go to school in Denver. Some school for kids like me." He forces a laugh.

"Oh."

We're both quiet for a minute. I pull at a thread on the gauze and Axel stares at the tiled floor.

"So, you can see the future, huh?"

I don't respond. I don't know if he's mocking me because he believes me or because he doesn't.

"It's none of your business, Axel. I was just trying to get us out of the fire. The fire that you started."

We stare at each other for a moment.

"I think it's cool that you can see the future like that," he says in a low voice. "I mean, I don't really get it, but it is weird how you drew that picture of Lyle and the cat and all that. Maybe if I could've seen the future I wouldn't have burned those stupid GI Joes on the bed up there and then I wouldn't be moving to Denver."

I don't respond. It doesn't seem to me like he'd need to see the future to figure that out. And he didn't need to be able to see more than one second ahead to know that pushing Lyle off his bike or punching him in the face was going to hurt him.

"I guess," I say. I want to yell at Axel for all the damage he's done, but my throat aches and I don't have the energy to squeak out more than a couple of words.

"Look," he says. "You saved me. I owe you for that." He stands up. There's something different about him. Maybe it's the bandage on his head or the way he's clutching the back of the chair as if he'd crumble without its support, but he looks broken. Seeing him so weak, I feel worse. Telling someone about the bullying wouldn't have only saved Lyle; it could have saved Axel, too.

"So, okay, I've gotta go," he says.

"Wait."

"What?" he asks after a minute.

I gesture out the window. "I see Jupiter. Do you see it?"

A small smile tugs at the corner of his mouth.

"I see Pluto," he says, and we both smile.

"Bye, Axel."

"Bye, Laney."

Axel follows the nurse out the door.

Shortly after, Walt steps back into the room. "Hey

there," he says. He's carrying a coffee in one hand and a large plastic bag in the other.

"Hey."

"You feel any better?"

"Maybe?" I say, coughing.

"You'll get there, honey." Walt sits on the side of my bed. "Look what I brought you." He opens the bag and tilts it toward me. It's full of dozens of cans of Play-Doh.

I fake a smile, but Walt's thoughtfulness just makes me feel worse.

"If I had just told someone, none of this would have happened," I say. Walt puts down the bag.

"Laney, we all make mistakes. But now you know. Something that serious, you need to tell an adult. Just, no more secrets, okay?" His expression changes when he realizes what he just said. Walt lets out a long sigh. Outside of my hospital room door, two doctors are talking. Their voices fade as they walk down the hallway.

Just a few days ago, Walt shoved the yellow note in his pocket to avoid talking about it with me. So much has happened since then that it's hard for me to even think straight. But we need to talk about it now.

"I know about your secret," I finally say.

"Listen, I want to talk to you about that. I should have told you about your mother. I know you found the note and—"

"How did you know?"

"I called you to check on you and you didn't answer. I kept calling and finally came home. When I got there, I found the house was empty and I saw the drawer in my room—" Walt's voice breaks. "I was just trying to protect you. I love you so much, and I didn't mean to hurt you. I didn't ever mean for you to find out like this."

Walt turns his back to me and clasps his head with his hands. It reminds me of that day on the stoop all those years ago.

"I remember when you found me," I say. "I didn't even know that you were my dad. I thought a stranger had left me, that you'd just found me . . ." I blink back tears and wipe my nose with the back of my hand.

"Laney, why didn't you tell me? Why didn't you tell me you thought that?" Walt stops and presses his lips together, breathing through his nose.

"I've always known you love me," I say, and now we're both crying. Walt gets up and grabs a tissue box from a table. We both blow our noses loudly at the same time and then can't help but laugh. Walt's smile disappears when he looks at my bandaged hand.

"Your mother, she knew this fire would happen. She was terrified of it. It's why she left. She couldn't bear the thought that she'd love you and then lose you. I didn't believe her. I thought it was just an excuse for her to leave me, to leave you . . . but I couldn't bear to tell you that she left for no reason either. And I was torn because I didn't believe her, and yet part of me must have because I was always so scared about you getting near fire. So I told you that she had died. It made me so mad at her when I told you that, but then you never really asked much about her. And now . . . I guess she was right about the fire after all."

"Not really," I say. "She wasn't really right. I'm here."

"It's true," Walt says with a small smile. "She was wrong about what would happen to you in the fire." He shakes his head. "It's odd, though. She did have these visions sometimes . . ."

"I do, too," I say quietly. "I saw the fire. That picture of Lyle I drew—"

"That scared me so much. It's why I kept asking you about it."

"It's not the only thing I've seen. I've had other visions over the years. Usually when I meet someone for the first time, but not always. Sometimes it just happens when I touch someone."

"I guess part of me always knew that, but I didn't want it to be true," Walt says. He pauses. "No more secrets?"

"No more secrets," I say, and I mean it. Hiding my future flashes from Walt was a mistake I won't make again.

"I love you, Laney."

I still have a million questions about my mom, but for now I let them go.

"I love you, too," I say.

Walt reaches over and squeezes my hand.

As soon as his hand touches mine, I close my eyes and find myself months into the future. I'm standing outside on a warm, breezy day, wearing a red dress and holding a bouquet of wildflowers—red columbines, wild lupines, and Indian paintbrushes tied with candy-red ribbon. Walt is standing next to me. His hair is clean of soot and, instead of his usual Carhartts and T-shirt, he's wearing a coat and tie. He winks at me and grins. I smile back and then look around me. My tree house is to my far right. I am in my own backyard, but it's been transformed. A white runner covered in red and white petals runs the length of our lawn, with chairs full of people seated on each side. At the end of the runner, Carmen, in a white sheath dress and sparkly silver shoes, stands arm in arm with her father. I know this scene. I've seen it before.

It's the same mix of people from town that I saw in my future flash years ago. Except something's different. Last time, I saw the people and the wedding, but it was more like I was watching a movie. I wasn't standing there wearing my red dress and holding a bouquet. And in the front row to my right, a freckle-faced boy with wild red hair smiles up at me. He's sitting next to a woman with pale red hair who is holding a striped gray cat on her lap. Lyle and his mom and Frida. They weren't here the last time I saw this, either.

I open my eyes.

"I saw something," I whisper to Walt. He pulls back to study my face. Then I see Carmen in the door behind him. She rushes over to me. I scoot over so that the three of us can sit squished together on the hospital bed.

"Oh, Laney, are you okay?" she asks me.

"I am."

She and Walt both glance at each other and offer up small smiles.

"Thanks for calling," I see Carmen mouth to Walt. He puts his hand over hers. She doesn't pull away.

"Laney was about to tell me about something she saw—" Walt catches himself.

"I get these images of the future," I explain to Carmen. "It's hard to describe, but sometimes I can see what's going to happen." It's funny, the lightness I feel telling Carmen my secret, and I find that the secret that's been bottled up inside of me for most of my life is suddenly easy to say out load.

Carmen raises both eyebrows.

"Well, what did you see?" she asks, without missing a beat.

"Yes," Walt says. "What did you see?"

I hesitate. "It's nothing," I say. This is something they should find out for themselves.

Walt gives me a look. "I thought we said no more secrets."

"This really isn't a secret. It's more of a surprise."

Walt starts to protest and Carmen joins in.

"Let's just say that I saw happiness," I say, smiling.

Walt and Carmen stare at each other for a moment as if mulling over whether to let me off the hook. "Well, I think we could all use a little happiness in our future, don't you think, Carmen?" Walt finally says, grinning.

"Of course," Carmen says. They both lean down to hug me.

Outside my hospital window, I see a prairie hawk, just like the one I saw that day on the hill when Lyle was attacked on his bike. A lot has happened since that day—a lot that I regret. I wish I had told someone about Axel sooner. I wish I had told Walt about my future flashes. I wish I had talked to him about how I remembered him finding me on the stoop. I wish my mother hadn't run away.

I look back at Carmen and Walt and decide to let all my regrets and wishes fly out the window and away with the wind. We've made mistakes, but I know now that it will all be okay. For the first time, I understand and appreciate the power of my gift. I can't change the past, but I can change the future.

Acknowledgments

Thank you to all of my friends and family. I couldn't have written this book without your love and support.

An extra huge thank-you to the following people:

- Melanie Gettier, for inspiring me to write about a girl who sees the future;
- Everyone in Eric Goodman's Advanced Novel workshop at the University of Iowa;
- Laura Oliver, for encouraging me to keep writing;
- My early readers: Carl Helmetag, Hannah McDonald, and Mollie McDonald;
- Shaun Bevins, editor extraordinaire;
- Patsy Helmetag, who read every single draft of

Future Flash. I have pages of notes from our phone calls, which would typically begin with me crying, "I'm stuck! Help!" Thank you for steering me through the rough patches;

- Elizabeth Prentiss Rao, who made the connection that made this book possible;

- Shannon Hassan, for seeing the potential in this story and taking the time to get it where it needed to be;

- My wonderful agent, Sarah Warner, at Warner Literary Group;

- Julie Matysik at Sky Pony Press, for your enthusiasm for this story;

- Everyone at Skyhorse Publishing for taking this manuscript and making it into a beautiful book;

- The Lago Mar ladies, whose stories have kept me laughing for over twenty years;

- My daughters' book clubs in Boulder, and all of the kids' book clubs around the world. Thank you for inspiring young readers to talk about books;

- My favorite readers, Eevee, Lucy, and Noni; and
- Toby, for always believing in me.

About the Author

———

Kita Helmetag Murdock resides in Boulder, Colorado, with her husband, three daughters, a dog named Gus, and a cat named Pip who regularly follows the girls to school and occasionally even breaks into their classrooms. Kita is the author of *Cecily Cicada* and *Francie's Fortune.* Visit her online at www.kitamurdock.com.